Doctor in Love

Also by Elizabeth Seifert

Young Doctor Galahad
(Winner of $10,000 Prize)
A Great Day
Thus Doctor Mallory
Hillbilly Doctor
Bright Scalpel
Army Doctor
Surgeon in Charge
A Certain Doctor French
Bright Banners
Girl Intern
Doctor Ellison's Decision
Doctor Woodward's Ambition
Orchard Hill
Old Doc
Dusty Srping
So Young, So Fair
Take Three Doctors
The Glass and the Trumpet
The Strange Loyalty of
   Dr. Carlisle
Hospital Zone
The Bright Coin
Homecoming
The Story of Andrea Fields
Miss Doctor
Doctor of Mercy
The Doctor Takes a Wife
The Doctor Disagrees
Lucinda Marries the Doctor
Doctor at the Crossroads
Marriage for Three
A Doctor in the Family
Challenge for Dr. Mays
A Doctor for Blue Jay Cove

A Call for Dr. Barton
Substitute Doctor
The Doctor's Husband
The New Doctor
Love Calls the Doctor
Home-Town Doctor
Doctor on Trial
When Doctors Marry
The Doctor's Bride
The Doctor Makes a Choice
Dr. Jeremy's Wife
The Honor of Dr. Shelton
The Doctor's Strange Secret
Legacy for a Doctor
Dr. Scott, Surgeon on Call
Katie's Young Doctor
A Doctor Comes to Bayard
Doctor Samaritan
Ordeal of Three Doctors
Hegerty, M.D.
Pay the Doctor
The Rival Doctors
Doctor with a Mission
To Wed a Doctor
The Doctor's Confession
Bachelor Doctor
For Love of a Doctor
A Doctor's Two Lives
Doctor's Kingdom
Doctor in Judgment
The Doctor's Second Love
Doctor's Destiny
The Doctor's Reputation
The Two Faces of Dr. Collier
The Doctor's Private Life
The Doctor's Daughter

DOCTOR
IN
LOVE

Elizabeth Seifert

DODD, MEAD & COMPANY

New York

F
Se Y   59450

ISBN: 0-396-06995-9
Library of Congress Catalog Card Number: 74-7770
Printed in the United States of America
by The Haddon Craftsmen, Inc., Scranton, Penna.

Doctor in Love

Chapter One

S T. Jerome's Hospital was entirely too large to be considered and accepted as a whole. One had to divide it into its component parts to comprehend it at all. The different units considered themselves as such—as small towns or suburbs of the "big city" that had fathered each one.

At some time in the remote past there must have been a single hospital, one which might be entered through a front door where there was a desk and someone to direct you to the surgery floor, or to the maternity ward, and so on.

Today each unit was in itself isolated, insulated from another. There was the Gynecology and Maternity Building, a Children's Hospital, a Renal Disease unit, and there was the Thoracic and Cardiovascular Building. On the upper floors of that handsome edifice of glass and steel and stone, there was the Thoracic and Cardiovascular Surgery Department. Here problems concerned with the heart, the lungs and the chest as a whole were examined, diagnosed, and solved if at all possible.

Here on a certain summer morning, as early as seven forty-five, an elderly man lay upon the table in Operating Room 3. He was a large man, yet, naked and under anaesthesia, he seemed strangely weak and soft.

The anaesthesiologist was arranging stands for intravenous feeding and transfusions. The scrub nurse, with swift, sure hands, laid out the instruments that would be needed—strings of hemostats, retractors, and suturing equipment.

In the corridor beyond O.R. 3, there was hurry, bustle, talk, even congestion. The elevators discharged nurses and doctors, stretchers bearing patients, orderlies pushing carts and containers. There was plan and order to the confusion, but confusion it was, just the same. Four of the five operating rooms were to be busy; it took teams of doctors, nurses, and technicians to do heart and lung surgery, to have everything ready and at hand when needed.

In O.R. 3, out of a loudspeaker high in the wall, drifted music from a local FM station. *Finlandia, Peer Gynt*—

Dr. Gordon Damery, who was to operate that morning, came in and spoke to his associate and to the senior house staff resident. "Good morning, Solley. How is your world today?"

"Good, I hope," said Dr. Solley, tall, his white cap tilted forward over most of his dark hair.

Dr. Damery nodded, went to the table and inserted a needle to monitor blood pressure. His quick, knowledgeable eye surveyed the whole scene—patient, equipment, and the people who were beginning to crowd the space available around the table. He left, and Dr. Solley painted the patient from chest to thigh with merthiolate. A nurse sprayed disinfectant from an aerosol can, and then the patient's nakedness disappeared under a blanket of green surgical sheets. Only the faintly orange chest and abdomen remained to be seen. Two surgical residents flanked the table as Dr. Solley grasped the first scalpel. From the loudspeaker woodwinds and strings, as well as a little brass, slipped into the *Valse Triste*. Dr. Solley said something lost within his face mask. One of the nurses at his elbow laughed.

Dr. Solley drew his knife down the chest. There was a thin line of blood. The assisting surgeon's hands moved in swiftly, tying off blood vessels, enlarging the incision. Dr. Solley called for the electric scalpel.

"To saw through the breastbone," one of the residents instructed the intern, in heart surgery for the first time that morning.

It was an hour later when Dr. Damery returned. The scrub nurse, Tillie—Miss Roberts—stood on tiptoe to assist him into a sterile surgical gown and rubber gloves. Within the incision, now big enough to hold a melon, the heart was identifiable as a mass of pulsing, crimson tissue.

An attendant had placed the artificial valve in a pan near Miss Roberts. The valve, to a layman, would look like three stainless steel objects with handles and shafts like screwdrivers; at one end was a cage mounted on a ring with sharp teeth. At the other end rested a hard plastic ball.

Now technicians rolled the heart-lung machine near Dr. Damery, and the busy surgeons plugged the patient into it to let the machine take over, oxygenating the blood, pumping it through the femoral artery in the thigh, taking in the dark blood from the venae cavae.

The music floated on, almost unheard above the click of instruments, the murmurs of the surgical team.

"Tie."

"Scissors."

"Blood pressure?"

"Tie."

Air conditioning erased all smell of anything; the air was chill and dry, so there was no need for the conventional brow mopping.

The surgeons removed the bad valve and replaced it, in minutes, with the artificial one. The heart-lung machine could be disconnected; the patient's own heart was ready to resume its duties. Dr. Damery left.

Dr. Solley and his assistnants closed the incision, and they too left, ready to go as a team to O.R. 5, where a woman awaited surgery.

The doctors knew what they would find; they were thoroughly familiar with the case. Here again would be the table, the instruments, the machine, the people—robed, gloved, and masked, set out like dolls to function, to perform.

But while making the transfer, Dr. Solley, a dedicated young surgeon, discussed the case with his team and the intern.

This was a housewife, he said, in her early forties, an active, alert person, married five years, who suddenly developed fatigue, lassitude, edema. She went for a checkup to a doctor who found the EKG unsatisfactory, and she was sent to a heart specialist. Thinking the condition the result of a childhood rheumatic fever, he advised rest for a month, then she was to go in for a full examination, even, possibly, catheterization. The ensuing diagnosis was a herniated mitral cord. After a delay of two weeks because of her father's critical illness, she had now come in, and

4

surgery for repair was to be done this day—a routine procedure.

The O.R. was ready, the patient was on the table, merthiolate was painted—and Dr. Solley, his eye on the monitors, sprang to attention. "Get Damery," he said firmly, not panicky.

"Crisis," the anaesthetist marked on the chart.

Down on the floor below surgery, in one of the small waiting rooms, reserved, and considered to be horror chambers by their occupants, sat the woman's husband, trying to sit still, trying to read one of the magazines spread out on the table, watching, watching the corridor and the elevator until the rims of his eyelids burned and he saw everything in a blur.

He groaned softly to himself, wiped the palms of his hands with a handkerchief, and sprang to his feet. It was too soon . . . Damery and Dr. Solley both had said four hours . . .

But here came the famous heart man, and with him the tall, dark-haired senior resident at his shoulder. Dr. Damery was a solid man, with a pleasant, eye-glassed face and keen blue eyes. Dr. Solley was quite tall; his thick, dark-brown hair grew from a peak on his forehead. He wore, nearly always, a pleasant, concerned expression on his face which he would have been surprised to hear called handsome. That noontime, both doctors still wore the shapeless o.r. suits, and their face masks dangled from an ear, their caps still were on their heads.

"We might as well get some lunch," Dr. Damery was saying.

". . . that poor woman," said Brook Solley.

"Here's the husband," Damery warned.

"Mr. Bailey," he said more loudly to the man whom they approached—a man whose face was flushed with dread, whose eyes begged them not to tell him . . .

"Your wife is all right," said Dr. Solley quickly, pitying the man's agony. Though why should he not be terrified, seeing the two surgeons approach him in this way?

"We had to abort the surgery," said Dr. Damery. "It is difficult to say just why your wife collapsed before we had made our first incision."

"It could have been a poor reception of the anaesthesia," suggested Dr. Solley.

Mr. Bailey's eyes went from one doctor's face to the other. "You didn't operate?" he stammered.

"We thought it best not to proceed," said Dr. Damery. "Shall we go back to the waiting room? A man can get trampled in these halls."

They did move to the waiting room. They sat down in the chairs and regarded each other.

"Tell me," said the frightened, mystified husband. "I thought—by now—"

"Yes. We too thought that, by now, we would have got far enough along in the surgery to know exactly what your wife's trouble is. But before—as I said—before we made the first incision, Dr. Solley here realized that the venal and the arterial blood did not balance. He and I together decided it best to let her come out of the anaesthesia. In six weeks or so, we can try again."

"But, my *God,* man!" cried the husband.

6

"It is most regrettable," said Dr. Solley.

"If she can't take an anaesthetic . . ."

"We'll explore the matter. We'll move very carefully," said Dr. Damery. "Another anaesthesia, perhaps."

"But this is serious?"

"It could be, yes. This morning, if it had been a matter of saving your wife's life, we might have proceeded. Many surgeons would have done so. But since the surgery was prescribed only to ensure health, not life, we thought it better to take a second look."

"Does she know?"

"Oh, no. She's in Recovery. By midafternoon, she'll begin to become aware . . ."

"And when she finds out . . ." cried Bailey. "I don't think she'll be able to go through all this again."

"It will be a shock," agreed Dr. Damery. "You, and we, must stand by to reassure her."

"I wish somebody would reassure me," cried the husband.

The doctors laughed. "We're a bit shaken, too," they told the layman.

"All the preparations—heart-lung machine—blood— Do you know that forty people from my company gave blood?"

"We do know."

"You scared me half to death, coming off that elevator, so solemn."

"I'm sorry, Bailey. But as we told you, this doesn't happen often."

"When can I see my wife?"

7

"At any time. She won't know you until later, but . . ."

"We'll take you up," said Dr. Solley.

The little procession they made was watched by everyone on that floor. By then, the story of the patient's collapse had traveled throughout cardiac. Murmurs of sympathy followed the men along the hall.

"If I were her, I'd not try it again," said a student nurse at the desk.

The Floor Head, a Special who happened to be present, and Mathilda Roberts, all turned fiercely on the girl. In five minutes the poor young thing had been given intensive instruction on attitude, patient relationship, and even on the way to tie her shoestrings.

"What goes on?" asked Dan Kearnes, leaning on the counter. "Has something happened that I missed?"

"That will be the day!" said the Special, going out into the hall again.

But Dan persisted. He was a reporter—a tall young man, brash, and often funny. Fun to talk to, to listen to. He regularly made the rounds of the hospital, getting feature stories. He especially liked items about prominent persons who might be patients—the actress upon whom a steel stage curtain had fallen, a prominent sports announcer smashed up in a car accident and now a patient in Orthopedics. Kearnes made all the departments. Sometimes he knew the story he wanted to get—a well-known police figure sick or injured, an unusual happening within the hospital itself. Perhaps a feud between staff and administration, a lottery prize won by an orderly, a projected

8

change in the hospital itself, a new building, new parking regulations . . .

One could find all sorts of stories in the big hospital complex. Dan's sources of information were many. His own quick eyes and ears, his nose for news, functioned well. He cultivated the interns, the nurses in training, any of the personnel with time to talk to him.

His favorite of all the personnel was Mathilda Roberts, o.r. nurse, and a cute chick if he ever had seen one, and he saw plenty. That morning he sensed a story in cardiac surgery; Tillie would know about it, and might be persuaded . . . though she didn't talk too readily about hospital matters.

But she did seem to have a little free time. She was a cute girl even when dressed for o.r. And it took a very cute girl indeed to look good in that outfit. What with the mop-cover hat, the long, shapeless gown, the sloppy shoes . . .

Besides, on this morning, Dan was bubbling with a news story of his own. He was dying to tell someone about it, and the someone of choice was Mathilda.

"Every reporter plans to write a book," he would lead into it. "Almost no reporter ever does write one. But me, I'm one in a thousand. I have written a book. And I have sold the book. So, let's celebrate!"

Things didn't go just the way he planned.

"Oh, hello, Dan," said Mathilda. "I can't talk now. This is my busy day."

She had a dust of freckles across her nose and cheeks. Even without lipstick or her hair showing, Mathilda was a pretty girl.

9

"How about a date?" Dan asked. "Then I can tell you about my book and the check I got."

She knew he'd been writing a book. She started down the hall. "It's just great about the book, Dan," she said over her shoulder.

He caught up with her.

"I have to be back on Surgical," she told him. He knew he was not allowed up there.

But he kept pace—and held the elevator door when she stepped into it. "How about having dinner with me to celebrate?" he asked.

"Sometime, maybe," said Mathilda, smiling at him.

"Sometime like tonight?" he asked eagerly.

"Look, Dan," she said. "I'm just as glad as can be that you've sold your book. And the Supe will kill us both if we hold this elevator. But I cannot decide on a date now. With four open hearts scheduled for today . . ."

She had other reasons to hesitate. She knew darn good and well that if she went on a date with Dan Kearnes, Brook Solley would go right up the wall. He considered himself engaged to marry Mathilda, and he thought Mathilda felt the same way. She did, of course. She really did. And she was happy about the arrangement. Brook was a fine man, and an especially fine doctor, conscientious about his work. He wanted everyone else to be that conscientious, too. His work came first with him, of course. He thought Mathilda understood that, just as he thought she knew he loved her, even if he often did not have much time to give her. Once on senior staff, of course, things would get easier.

Should she ask Brook if he'd mind her having this kind

of date with Dan? The poor fellow was really keyed up about his book. And Brook knew, or should know, that *he* came first with her.

So why not dinner with Dan that evening? Brook would not be free.

And surely she could afford to be nice to this chap. She remembered her high school senior prom. A less than really desirable boy had invited her, and she had refused, waiting for the better offer which she felt sure would come, and which did come. But she had always regretted that choice. The less-than-desirable was a nice kid, and it wouldn't have hurt her . . .

It wouldn't hurt her now.

She smiled at Dan. "Ride up with me," she said. "Tell me where we'll have dinner."

Brook saw them. He saw the elevator open, Mathilda come out, with Dan Kearnes inside. They laughed and said things to each other before the elevator door closed.

Brook was in ICU—in the "fishbowl"—attending to Mrs. Bailey, "that poor woman." He had sent the husband down for lunch or coffee; the doctor would stay around, though he was due in o.r. again in twenty minutes. And so was Tillie. She would be there, of course. She knew her job, and did it, always. If she had a fault, it was that she was too interested in people. And perhaps that was not a fault at all.

Brook Solley, on his part, was too serious. About everything. He recognized this, and loved Tillie for her outgoing ways, for the fun she could have, for her friendly nature. He told her that she talked too much, even while

11

he envied her because she could.

Now he checked on Mrs. Bailey's vital signs, touched the skin of her bare arm, turned and checked on the other patient of that morning, the man with the new heart valve. Both were doing well, and, slipping out of the gown, dropping the mask, he went out into the hall—with his usual look back through the windows at the room which he had just left. Two nurses and a resident were in watchful attendance.

He went to the desk to check, as Mathilda was doing, on the surgical schedule. Both knew what the next case was to be, a young boy with calcium deposits. Both knew that in five minutes they were due in scrub.

But they checked. "How's Mrs. Bailey?" Mathilda asked.

"All right. I hope I might be around when she comes out."

"She might take off and run."

Brook nodded. "I hope we can reassure her."

"You will. Is she a nice person?"

Dr. Solley looked over his shoulder. The nurse was bending over Mrs. Bailey. "Why, yes," he said. "I think so. She's attractive. Talks well. She and her husband are both bright and intelligent people." He gave these details slowly, thoughtfully.

"He's a space engineer, isn't he?"

"Now, Tillie . . ."

She grinned. "Look. I am not Dan Kearnes. Did you know he'd sold his book?"

Brook started down along the hall; Mathilda stayed at his elbow.

12

"Has he?" asked the doctor, without any great interest.

"You don't sound very excited."

"Look, Tillie . . ."

"I'm excited. For Dan, I am. It's a wonderful thing to write a book and know it will be published. He wants to celebrate, and I can understand that."

"Now, how would he . . .?"

Tillie laughed. She had a pleasant, pretty laugh, almost childlike in its clarity. "I believe a half-bottle of wine would do it," she admitted.

Brook turned his shoulder to push through to the doctors' dressing room.

"I'd think you could be just a little excited, too," Mathilda told him.

Brook looked down at her, and his eyes smiled. "You're like a kid," he said. "Are you telling me that Kearnes has asked you for a date to share his half-bottle of wine?"

"Well, yes," said Mathilda, "he did." She jiggled from one foot to the other, and she leaned toward Brook, wanting him to understand, to share . . .

Someone within the half-open door spoke to Dr. Solley. Sharply he asked questions. "Why? How long?" He turned back to Mathilda. "This isn't our day," he murmured. "There's a fifteen-minute hold. Some idiot fouled up on tubing size. I'll go look at Mrs. Bailey again."

Mathilda watched him stride down the corridor and turn into Intensive. From the set of his shoulders, his head, the way his gown tail snapped around his knees, she knew that Brook was upset.

He didn't want her to have a date with Dan. Poor Dan. She'd wait, and persuade Brook . . .

13

He came back within minutes. "Mrs. Bailey is all right," he said. "But I am getting more and more concerned. I talked to the resident about when she wakes up."

"And finds she doesn't have any bandages," Tillie agreed.

"It will be a shock."

"You bet it will!" said Tillie.

"And now we may decide that we must catheterize to be more sure of what we have. That's pretty rugged, Tillie."

"Yes," she agreed. "It is."

"Let's go have some coffee."

Both glanced at the wall clock.

"They'll page us," Brook reminded her. "They'll page the whole crew."

She nodded, and they crossed the corridor to the small lounge. Mathilda put the paper cups into the holders. Brook lifted the carafe. "This stuff is pure poison," he warned her.

There was one other person in the room, a doctor who seemed to be asleep. Miss Roberts and Dr. Solley chose a small table and chairs as far from him as was possible.

Tillie stirred sugar into her cup. "I think I have to go on this date, Brook," she said softly.

"Why? Kearnes can drink a half-bottle of wine by himself."

"What sort of celebration would that be? Besides, he says I helped him with his book."

"How could . . . ?" Brook stiffened. "*Did* you?" he asked sharply.

Mathilda shook her head. "I can't see how."

14

"Well, *I* can figure out a few ways. Plenty happens around here. Enough to make several books. Take the case we had this morning."

"Mrs. Bailey?"

Brook glanced across at the sleeping doctor. "Shhhh," he cautioned. "But, yes. A writer could build something around that. Then take the row that's going on with the courtesy doctors wanting more rights. Priority rights on beds, you know, as well as the use of o.r., lab services, and other facilities."

"Staff doctors have priority," Mathilda murmured. "Courtesy ones have to wait their turn."

"And they don't like that to be so exclusive. There's some hassle about e.r. duty, too, ward rounds, and committee meetings. If you'd tell Kearnes about those fights, he could use them."

"Well, I didn't tell him anything at all about the rows you doctors get into."

Brook was watching her. He liked to do that. "If you told him anything at all . . ." he mused.

The enunciator crackled, and they both looked up. But it was a page for an orderly needed on 11. Surgery was on 12. Offices, diagnostics and therapy were on 10.

Mathilda touched Brook's hand. "I didn't tell Dan a thing!" she insisted. "I don't talk about hospital matters."

"I certainly hope not, dear."

She smiled at him; she stroked his hand. "I'd rather have a date with you," she murmured.

"I'm on thirty-six-hour duty."

"I know you are. But I'd still rather . . ."

He took her hand in his and held it.

15

A nurse came in and woke the sleeping doctor. They both spoke to Tillie and Brook.

"What happened in One this morning?" the doctor asked.

Brook told him, briefly, about Mrs. Bailey.

"I believe I would have gone on," said the other surgeon.

Brook nodded. "We could have. Damery said no."

"Then I guess it had to be no. But I'd bet you won't get the lady back on the table again."

Brook shrugged. "Not me, perhaps. But I'll bet on Damery."

The nurse got her doctor away, and Tillie and Brook were alone. He leaned across the table and kissed her. "I know I'm jealous," he confessed, "but I do love you, Tillie. I've asked you to marry me."

She nodded, her eyes smiling. "Yes," she said softly, "you have."

Dr. Solley straightened. "Has Kearnes asked you?"

Tilley made a small sound of surprise and exasperation. "Oh, *no!*" she cried. "Nothing of the sort. He doesn't— He wouldn't, Brook! There's never been anything of that kind. And tonight won't be a real date. He just asked me to have dinner. He wants a chance to tell me about this book he's written, and to show me the check he got."

"An advance, it's called," said Brook. "Don't you know —hasn't he told you what the book is about? I mean, he's always around. Surely he has told you."

"Only that he was writing a book. I am just guessing that it has a hospital or medical angle."

"Well—" The loudspeaker burst out, and it was very

16

loud. "O.R. Three team report . . ."

Brook grabbed Tillie's hand, and they ran, leaving their coffee cups behind on the table. Somebody would fuss about that. There would be a bulletin board notice, and notes in the mailboxes, and—

By seven o'clock that evening, Miss Roberts, scrub nurse and o.r. Head for the team of Solley and Damery, was tired from a day's full schedule of surgery. She knew better than anyone that she should not be going on a dinner date. A light dinner at the hospital cafeteria, home, a hot bath, and bed, would be better—much better.

As things were—She had escaped the hospital as soon as she possibly could. The last o.r. check, thank goodness, had gone smoothly, and there had been no chance for arguing further with Brook.

He was in ICU talking to Mrs. Bailey, who was pretty well conscious after the noontime events. Though he would not have said much more than he had said in the lounge, Mathilda knew he would rather she did not go on this date.

And to be truthful, at that minute she would rather not, too.

She let herself into her small apartment, relishing its quiet. By habit, she set out shoes and uniform for the next morning, or for some emergency call, though, barring a disaster of major proportions, members of a heart surgery team would not be called after a full day in surgery.

She had already decided what she would wear for dinner with Dan. Nothing fancy. A simple shift of tan linen, with some Indian-looking embroidery on the yoke. She took a quick shower, brushed her hair hard—it was brown so close to red that often she was called "Red." It had a natural wave that was a blessing for which she constantly thanked Mother Nature. She found comfortable shoes—red ones—and hoped that, for five minutes, she could stretch out in her big armchair.

She could not. The girl in the next apartment came to borrow shampoo, and to talk.

Yes, Mathilda had had a long day. Yes, she had a date. Not Dr. Solley. He would be on call duty all night. Her date was due any minute.

The girl finally left, and the telephone rang. It was Mathilda's mother, long distance, saying that she hadn't heard . . .

Oh, Lord!

"Mother, I am sorry! I guess there just wasn't anything to write about."

Yes, she was fine. Busy, yes. No, she wouldn't have a vacation until August. How was the rest of the family?

Dan arrived, and Mathilda stretched the telephone cord to open the door for him. "My mother," she whispered, covering the telephone mouthpiece, a maneuver she never entirely trusted to ensure privacy.

But, finally, her mother hung up, and Mathilda said "Hello" to Dan. Was she dressed all right? They weren't going anywhere fancy?

He mentioned an Italian restaurant.

Mathilda looked down at her dress—doubtfully.

"You look fine," Dan assured her. "You always look fine."

She smiled at him and searched for her purse. She

18

couldn't locate it. "In a place the size of a phone booth," she protested, "you wouldn't think I could lose anything!"

The purse was found, wedged into the corner of the couch. "Just where I left it," said Mathilda brightly. Did Dan want a drink?

Her mother had asked her about Brook. What would she have said if Mathilda had told her she was having a date that evening with another young man? Plenty! Mathilda smiled to think of all her mother would have found to say. She would have come right through the telephone; that's what she would have done. Mrs. Roberts considered an engagement as binding as matrimony. "But, Mother, there is no formal engagement!" No ring, no definite plans. Six months ago, at Christmastime, Dr. Solley had asked Mathilda to marry him. Senior house staff resident, who would go on senior staff the next year, they could have been married right away. But Mathilda had wanted to pay back, herself, every penny of the money she had borrowed for her training. They would, and could, wait until this debt was cleared. But she was going to marry Brook; she was sure that she loved him. And maybe she should not be going on a date with another man.

Chapter Two

WELL," she said finally, "I think we can get away now—if we hurry." She smiled up at Dan. He had come close to her, and she knew he wanted to kiss her. She shook her head.

"No!" she confirmed the gesture. "That wasn't part of the arrangement."

"Okay," Dan conceded. He opened the door. Mathilda looked around the single room of her home. It was a large room, with three windows that looked out across the city. There was a brown velvet couch which made into a bed, a big armchair, and two smaller chairs. Turquoise painted walls and brown, turquoise and yellow curtains. Her starched white cap was on the table. Behind a row of shuttered doors was a small bath, a clothes closet, and a tiny kitchen. It was a small, pleasant place.

Perhaps she should have fixed something here; she could have had Dan bring steaks and his bottle of wine.

She shook her head and went to the door, her hand on the light switch. No, sir! The place was too small, too intimate. Sometimes she did fix dinner for Brook, but that was different. He was different.

Now, at home . . .

Waiting for the elevator, replying to Dan's chatter, she thought swiftly of her home on such an evening, of the small town where she had grown up and gone to school, of the comfortable house where her mother had always enjoyed preparing dinner for her daughters' dates—something special added to the family dinner, or, on occasion, the whole dinner special.

The boys, the young men would come to the house, freshly barbered, freshly groomed from their smootheddown cowlicks to the tips of their polished shoes, their cheeks pink, their eyes a little anxious. Mathilda's father would admit them and talk to the boys about engineering until "supper" was ready.

Almost never had a boy been interested in engineering, but it was the only thing Bruce Roberts knew or cared anything about. He was engineer at the town water and power plant, a responsible position.

Dan jiggled Mathilda's elbow. "Hey!" he cried. "Where have you got to?"

She looked up at him. "I'm sorry," she said. "I was thinking about home. You know, my mother called just before you came. If I'd never moved to the big city, she would cook dinner for you tonight. A pork roast, sweet potatoes, and pecan pie."

Dan laughed. "Sounds good. Fattening, but delicious."

The restaurant, entered through an arched doorway, past a small fountain, up a curving flight of stone steps, was a place of dim lights and soft music. The guests were greeted by a maitre d', dressed formally.

"I told you I wasn't dressed up," Mathilda whispered to Dan.

He pressed her shoulder.

Their small table was next to a railing which overlooked

21

the small dance floor; there were candles in wrought-iron holders—and an obsequious wine waiter.

Dan ordered the wine after some lengthy discussion.

"It's too expensive," Mathilda told him when the order was completed.

"This is a celebration, remember?"

A waiter came, slender, dark-haired, dark-mustached.

"I happen to know he's Persian," Mathilda murmured, opening the huge menu.

"Have you been here before?" asked Dan.

"Yes. Dr. Damery took the whole team to dinner here when this place first opened. They have strolling musicians. Or did."

They still did have them. A guitar, two violins—and they played the *Hora,* which made Mathilda laugh aloud. "That's *Italian?*" she asked.

"I'm glad I don't know one tune from another," said Dan. "You're sure you want scampi?"

"I'm sure. But I would like antipasto first. They serve a huge plate of it, and I'm starved."

They had their antipasto, they drank the wine, and ate the food. "It's really very good," said Dan critically.

"It should be at this price," Mathilda reminded him. "And I know I sound small-town. Mainly because I am small-town."

"You're delicious, too," said Dan.

But he wouldn't talk about the book. "Not yet," he said.

They danced, they came back to the table, and Mathilda watched the waiter serve Dan's veal and her scampi. She gazed at Dan—and thought about Brook. The two men were different, and yet somewhat alike. That was why

22

both appealed to Mathilda, she decided. Dan could have been a few years the younger of the two; his manner certainly was more brash. He lacked Brook's air of sure competency.

But Dan also had dark hair—straight, smooth, worn a little long on his neck and about his ears. He had a nice face, with conventional features, a well-formed mouth, a round chin. Brook's chin jutted and dug a deep line below his rather large mouth. Dan's nose was short and straight; Brook's was on the large side. Dan had nice brown eyes, Brook's were a surprising blue-green, steady and thoughtful.

The night Dr. Damery had entertained the heart team here in this restaurant, Mathilda had worn a long skirt, and discovered that Brook Solley was a very good dancer. The other women had made that discovery, too, but Mathilda . . .

"You know," said Dan now, "you dance exceptionally well, Tillie."

It was a nickname which Mathilda hated. Brook used it, and that was all right, but—

"You said you were going to tell me about the book," Mathilda reminded him when they returned to their table.

"I shall."

"When? You know, I don't believe there is a book."

"Oh, but there is, sweetheart. There definitely *is!* I wrote it, and it's been accepted for publication."

"Was it that good?"

He laughed. "I hope it's good," he said. "But honesty makes me admit that the first publisher didn't jump at it."

"Though another one did."

23

"Yes. And of course this one must be better, to use such good judgment."

Mathilda laughed. Between them, they laughed quite a bit. Dan was excited, and she always tried to match a date's mood. But—"I really can't stay out late," she reminded him. "Seven A.M. comes around just like that!" Her fingers wouldn't snap and she laughed at that. Dan did, too, rather noisily.

Mathilda pushed her chair back. "We've had enough wine and garlic," she declared. "Time to go home."

"Aw, Tillie!"

"Don't call me Tillie. And if you won't take me, I know the way."

"Okay," he conceded. "That's the trouble with smart girls." He signaled for the check.

But when he drove her home, he stopped at his apartment house, not Mathilda's. She sat stubbornly in the car seat. "You've lost your way," she told him.

"No, I haven't. I live here. On the third floor." He gestured up to the tall, shining windows.

"I believe you live here," she assured him. "That's what is wrong."

He turned so that he could look into her face. His car was low-slung, and the top was down. "Are you afraid of Solley?" he asked. "Doesn't the guy trust you?"

Mathilda tied her red scarf around her hair. "I don't know," she said.

"You don't *know?*"

She lifted her chin. "The matter has never come up!" she said spunkily.

"But you hope he doesn't."

24

Mathilda laughed. "I'll have to think about that, won't I?" she asked.

"Will you come upstairs with me?" he asked, almost pleadingly. "I'll be the perfect gentleman."

"Yes, you will be," she said. She was gazing up at the face of the apartment.

The windows were in banks of four—high, narrow ones. First floor, second, third, and the fourth floor hooded by an arch of stone work.

Outside, before the lowest row of windows, lounged a couple—a young man and a girl, both in white shorts, white sneakers. The man's sweater was white, banded in blue and red, the girl's was dark blue. They talked earnestly, intimately.

"They play tennis late, don't they?" said Mathilda mildly.

"We have an inside court. Two courts, in fact. Come inside and I'll show you. The social rooms are on the first floor, and there are always people about."

"I doubt if they would notice if you'd stop being a gentleman," said Mathilda, but she prepared to step out of the car.

"Is this one of those swinging-singles places?" she asked, looking about the main room of the "social" area. There were couches, big chairs, a fountain—and people who didn't give them a second glance.

Dan showed her the tennis courts, the swimming pool, the billiard room.

Mathilda was interested and amused. No, she cried, she would not want to live there. "I wouldn't qualify, I'm sure. I'm a working girl, remember, and the work I do is too

25

hard; I get too pooped. To date, I am single, but my swing almost never gets off the ground."

"Will you come up to my pad?" he asked. "I'll leave the door open."

She looked at her watch. "Twenty minutes," she agreed. "And leaving the padlock off would do nicely."

His apartment was on the third floor, and it was small, pleasant, and not at all frightening. Mathilda shook her head at his offer of a drink. "Just show me the book," she said.

"Well, of course, the *book* is in New York. I can show you the carbon copy." He went over to the desk and put his hand on a thick folder. Now he seemed nervous, less confident of himself. "I can show you the contract."

He gave Mathilda the document, and she sat down on the front edge of a chair to look at it. Red printing, black printing—there was Dan's name—DANIEL KEARNES—there was the name of the book—MAKE YOUR PLAY. She said the name aloud and looked across the room to Dan and smiled.

With a flourish, he took out his billfold and produced a check, brought it across the tweed carpet to Mathilda. A blue check, signed and countersigned, the publisher's name imprinted.

She was impressed. "But that's wonderful, Dan!" she said. "That's quite a lot of money."

"It certainly is," he agreed. "Of course we don't know if the sales will pay them back . . ." He was making an effort to be offhand, but he was really excited. His fingers were damp, his brown eyes shone, and there were spots of red on his cheeks.

26

She saw the way his hand shook when he put the check away.

Mathilda stood up and said she must get home. She—

"Yes," he agreed. "I'll take you. And thanks for the evening, Tillie."

"Well, thank *you!*"

"I'll keep in touch with you. I won't be coming to the hospital regularly any more. You see, I've quit my job."

She was shocked. "But, Dan!" she protested. "Should you have done that?"

He shrugged. "I hope so. Anyway, I've already quit."

"Oh, Dan—"

They still were discussing the wisdom of the step, always moving slowly toward the door, when the telephone rang.

It was just that. The sharp, brief ring of the telephone on the desk, repeated as Dan strode toward it, quieted when he answered.

Mathilda stayed where she was, waiting. He surely would not be long.

She smoothed the front of her linen dress, she looked at the cover of the magazine on the end table—then, frowning a little, she began to watch Dan's face as he talked. His expression was such—surprise, even dismay, perhaps a little protest . . .

Who could be calling?

She began to listen, and her puzzlement mounted with each thing he said. "But, sir, I can't do that!"

"No, sir."

"Yes, sir."

"Well, of course I want to be cooperative."

27

"Certainly I know the terms of our agreement."

Something was wrong. But what? And how wrong?

Mathilda moved closer, listening intently, watching his face. He kept saying, "Yes, sir." "No, sir."

And finally, he concluded the conversation with a resigned "All right, sir. I'll be there."

Before he had put the phone down, Mathilda was ready to spring at him.

"What *was* it?" she cried. "You look terrible. Was it your publisher? Or maybe your long-lost wife? No. You wouldn't say 'No, sir' to any wife. Would you?"

Dan gave her a sickly grin, went around her and into his tiny kitchen, Mathilda close at his shoulder.

"I should have taken you home sooner," he said, feebly attempting a joke. He reached for a glass, he took ice cubes from a tray and splashed whisky over them. He didn't offer anything to Mathilda.

With her still closely following, he went back to the living room and stood gazing out of the window, now and then gulping the whisky. The glass shook in his hand, and the ice tinkled. Once he leaned his forehead against the window glass.

Mathilda watched him in great concern. "If I could do anything . . ." she said helplessly.

He smiled at her, drained the glass, then put his hand on her shoulder.

She looked up at him. "Are you all right, Dan?"

"Sure I'm all right. That was the Administrator on the phone. The hospital administrator, you know?"

Mathilda fell back a step. "The—*What* hospital administrator?" she asked, unbelieving.

28

"Yours. St. Jerome's."

The head administrator? The big wheel? "Mr. Fichter?" she cried. *"He* called you? But he couldn't, Dan. Somebody's kidding you. Fichter doesn't work this late. He just never does. Not unless the joint burns down. He . . ." She was babbling, and Dan waited for her to run down.

"I don't know if he was still at his office," he said then. "But it was Mr. Fichter, and he wants to see me. Tomorrow."

"Oh, gee whiz! Maybe he's going to stop your coming to the hospital. He sometimes doesn't like publicity stories about us. He . . ."

Dan took her arm firmly in his hand. "Mathilda . . ." he began.

"Why does he want to see you, Dan?" she asked, beginning to be really worried.

"Not to stop a reporter from going around the hospital halls. I told you I've quit my job."

Yes, he had told her. But Fichter . . .

Privately, Mathilda thought the administrator was a stuffed shirt. She'd never had any direct contact with the man. Not any at all. She knew her job, and she did it. The Supervisor took care of any business between Thoracic Surgery and the main office. If Mathilda needed anything or had any complaints, she went to the Supe.

Of course she knew Mr. Fichter by sight. He presided at the hospital Christmas parties, and made a speech before gifts and bonuses were passed out. His speech was never anything much. She had to think he was a better administrator than speaker, and he probably was. They had a good hospital, and the "plant" was always expanding or going in for innovations.

Mr. Fichter was a round man, not tall. By means of sunlamp or golf, he kept a good tan on his skin, including his balding head. He regularly made rounds of the hospital units. Mathilda had seen him standing against the wall of the observation room in the heart theater.

Tonight . . .

"What did he want? What does he want to see you about?" she asked faintly. This was all getting beyond her.

"Well, it's about my book," said Dan.

"Your . . . ? *What* about your book, Dan?"

"Well, you see, it has a medical setting, and it's about doctors and things. I know the publishers were checking names of doctors who practice here in the city. I was clear there, of course. Don't stare at me that way, Tillie!"

She brushed her hand across her eyes. "Go on," she said. "Tell me."

"I am telling you." He walked away from her, turned and came back. "It seems that the publishers—to protect themselves, I suppose—from libel suits and all that—I suppose they have checked the main theme of my book— it's a novel, of course—with the newspaper where I worked. And then they've checked it with the hospitals which I have been covering."

"St. Jerome's?"

"That's one of them."

"And all this is about your book?" She sounded incredulous.

"I'm afraid so," said Dan.

"But why?" she asked intently. "Did they decide your book was about us? About St. Jerome's?"

30

"Well, yes, I think they did."

"But—I don't understand. The office usually likes publicity about the hospital. Doesn't it?"

"Oh, yes. Or I would not have been allowed to make my rounds."

"That's what I figured. Then what's the problem?"

"Well, it seems the hospital likes what Fichter calls controlled publicity."

"Huh?" She was staring again. "I don't understand. In fact, I don't understand anything about all this. You are talking way over my head." She sat down on the couch, not looking at her watch. Her twenty minutes had long since passed.

Walking about the room, then sitting beside her, turned to face her, Dan tried to explain. He himself, he admitted, was still new and green about this book writing business. "Of course I know about reporting," he explained. "I've been in that for ten years. Longer, if you count what I did at the university. Well, anyway. The book I've written is a novel, and it is fiction. And I don't suppose the publishers would have got in touch with Mr. Fichter or any hospital if I had not been a special feature writer, visiting the hospitals regularly. I probably should not have told them that."

"They could easily have found it out," said Mathilda quietly.

"Yes, I suppose they could. There is a great difference, you know, between the story a reporter will tell and a work of fiction he may write. In the first capacity, he deals with facts; in the second, he makes up the story."

"Then what's the problem?"

31

"Oh, the hospital—Mr. Fichter—is touchy about any sort of writing that could or might involve patients of his hospital."

"But you do write about patients. You did that story on the boy born with the external heart."

"Yes, with the whole Thoracic staff checking on each detail, even the way I spelled terms."

"Is that what Mr. Fichter plans to do tomorrow? Check on your spelling?"

Dan tried to laugh. "I wish I could think so. No, I believe he'll want to learn enough about the book to decide if my story could be identified as being about any of his patients."

"It couldn't be, if you made up the whole thing."

"Oh, Tillie, you don't understand."

She stood up. "You're right there, Buster. I don't know when I've understood a subject less. But now, before we start for my place, I'll tell you what I'd do. I wouldn't go near Mr. Fichter tomorrow."

He looked up at her in amazement. "But, Tillie!" he cried. "I have to go. Maybe nothing will come up. I don't know. But—the publishers would tell me to go, if Fichter appealed to them. Nobody wants a libel suit, of course."

"How could there be a libel suit?"

"Well—I suppose—" He rumpled his hair with his fingers, then smoothed it. "Now, there's this," he said. "I'll try again to explain. You know—you will remember —telling me of a little happening in the hospital . . ."

She could feel the blood drain from her face, she could feel her hands go cold.

"You said today," she gasped, "that I had helped

32

you . . ." And Brook had been angry at the suggestion that she had.

"But you did, Tillie! You have."

"Don't call me Tillie. And *what* have I told you?"

"Oh, about a patient going for a stroll on the grounds, wearing only his hospital shirt. About the child you made a canvas jacket for because she scratched at her incision."

Tillie stared at him. "Little funny happenings like that, you mean? A woman afraid to take red pills . . . Dan Kearnes, you can't write a *book* about such things! Naming a baby Mercurochrome—things like that!"

"A writer can use them, dear. For background. Like the color incidents you get when you watch a televised football game. But in your case, there was one story you gave me—just the bare bones of it, of course."

"*I* gave it to you?"

"Yes, you did. Oh, only a word or two. But they attracted my interest. Then I asked around, and got some angles. Gradually I filled in the story. Slanted it, naturally. That's where the fiction part comes in. Reporting, you have to tell it straight. With fiction, you take the bones and add your own padding. You guess, and tell, how the matter—the affair—works out, for one thing. You . . ."

Mathilda was devastated. Completely. She hoped, she prayed, Dan would not tell her what bare bones of what story she had given him. That she should not—Oh, she *knew* she talked too much! She knew that, and she did try to keep still the way Brook did, all quiet, firm, and dignified. But that just wasn't Mathilda!

She liked people, and, especially when she was sorry for a person, she would talk to them, and about them.

33

Though why she should ever have been sorry enough for Dan Kearnes, for this—this *swinger* . . .

What *could* she have said to him? *What* story was the man talking about? Maybe she had not been the one to tell him! Oh, she hoped so! Brook would be furious if it turned out . . .

She well remembered his reaction when she'd said that Dan claimed she had helped him write his book.

That day—this morning? Yes, it was, but it seemed at least a week ago. But—this morning—the Bailey case had gone sour—Well, not *sour,* of course. But they couldn't proceed, and that gave the team extra time, and she and Brook, while waiting to be told that things were ready and they could proceed with the next case, had gone into the lounge . . .

Dr. Usher had been snatching a nap there. He was a resident surgeon and probably had been up all night. A nurse came in to get him—and Brook had read the riot act to Mathilda about talking too much. The coffee machine had bubbled, and the enunciator had broken out a time or two—Brook had gone off once to check on Mrs. Bailey—

That patient probably had wakened completely by now and had been told that she had not had the surgery— which meant that she would have to go through the whole scene again, poor thing. Mathilda could guess how she would feel. If things could go wrong one time, they could another. Why, her story alone would give Dan material— or she supposed it could.

She pulled at Dan's sleeve. "Tell me *what* story you think I gave you, Dan," she said. "I've got to go home to bed. But I won't sleep a wink until I know—so tell me.

What bare bones of what story did I tell you?"

"I thought you'd know."

"I haven't the slightest idea."

He told her, or enough that she knew the case in hand. And, knowing, she really did shiver. She went over to the window, seeing the room reflected in its glass, and Dan behind her, talking, gesturing, herself a dark silhouette against the lamplight.

He told it all. Enough, at any rate. He mentioned the personalities, and the way men got touchy and notional, their judgment influenced by personal affairs. Oh, yes, she knew the case! Had she said much? No. Dan said he'd "asked around." He'd padded and built up the characters, and made up the story. How near the truth would that be?

Now that she knew what skeleton of what story she had sketched out for him, she was more upset than ever. Would she have to tell Brook Solley about this enormous thing which she had done? She need not. If anything at all developed, he would know that she was involved from what she already had told him—about the book, and all.

It wasn't that she was afraid of Brook. But she certainly did not want to displease him!

She tried desperately to recall just what she had told Dan about the Sherwins. She had not mentioned names; she was sure of that. And she could not have told him anything about background or subsequent developments. He'd have had to guess, or make up, all of those things.

She said something of this sort to him now. And he agreed quickly, even brightly. "Oh, yes!" he said eagerly. "That's the art of fiction writing. You take the skeleton of a story, or maybe just an idea, and around it you build live people and real-seeming, logical events. They probably are more alive than what actually happened. You can't use improbabilities, you know, or coincidence. And real life is full of those things."

Curiously, Mathilda looked at him. Dan, quite evidently, was still very pleased with himself, and happy in his role of an author.

She sighed and moved toward the door. "Will you take me home now?" she asked.

"Aw, Tillie, why should you leave? It's still early."

"It is past ten o'clock, and if I'm in trouble, as it seems I am, I'll need enough time—hours, even—to think about it."

"How are you in trouble?" He was honestly asking that question.

"Well, it seems pretty clear to me, Dan. If you talk to the Administrator tomorrow— Do you know him?"

"Well, sure I know him. I've never drunk a beer with him or anything like that, but when I've prepared a story about St. Jerome's, it often needed cooperation from his office, and of course clearance there, too."

"Did you see him, or just someone in his office? It's a rather big office, if you take in the whole operation."

"Yes, I know that. And you're right. Often I dealt with an assistant, or left a script with his secretary—things like that. But, yes, I have dealt with Mr. Fichter in person."

"All right. He—well, he didn't get where he is, or hold his important job, by being a softy."

"No. I realize that, and that's why I've been upset myself to know that I'd have to see him tomorrow."

"I could tell you about some hatchet jobs he's done,

36

both to get where he is and to stay there." Her face flushed. "But I hope I've learned my lesson. I don't tell you anything, ever again!"

"Aw, Tillie! I mean, Mathilda."

"Mr. Fichter is a very smart man, Dan. He knows how to get the information he wants. I had hoped never to come anywhere near him, or risk the chance of his office being concerned with me."

"But—"

"Yes, you can too involve me. Tomorrow you will see Mr. Fichter, and talk to him about your book, and I'll bet just anything, one way or another, you'll tell him where you got the skeleton, or the bare bones, or whatever, for your novel. And the next thing you know—I'll know it even sooner—I'll be out of a job. And that's not good, Dan Kearnes. It isn't good at all." She could hear the anger and the fear shrill in her voice. Well, she *was* angry, and she was afraid.

Dan came over to her, and when he would have touched her, she drew away from him.

"I won't tell Fichter a thing that could hurt you, Mathilda," he said earnestly.

"Yes, you will, Dan. You'll talk. You're a great talker, you know. You're excited about the book, and nobody could blame you, but you'll say a lot of things or even just start to say them, and somewhere you'll say you got the bones of your story from a nurse, and they'll guess the rest."

He laughed at her fears, he tried to cajole her into being sensible. Finally he tried to cuddle her—and she refused his efforts angrily.

37

"You're mad at me, Mathilda," he said in a teasing tone. "You should know I wouldn't hurt you for anything on earth. I am very fond of you, and if it weren't for Brook Solley—"

"Will you please leave Brook out of this?" she flashed at him. "He didn't want me to have a date with you tonight, and now I know he was right!"

"Does he have the right to tell you what people you can see?"

"Oh, you know this was more than that! All that food and wine—it was a *date!* And Brook does have a right to advise me on such things. He wants to marry me, and he's going to be so—so—so *angry*—when he knows about the trouble over your book—when he knows you've involved me—"

"He won't know, Mathilda. I promise you he won't. Besides, you're not in trouble, and you won't be. Do you think I'd mention your name?"

"I don't know. I hope you wouldn't. Not directly. But so far as Brook is concerned, I've already said to him that you claimed I'd given you the story idea for your book."

"But how and why would you say such a thing to Dr. Solley?" Again Dan was surprised and frankly curious.

"Well, this morning—way back then, when you asked me for a date to celebrate the sale of your book and you told me I was responsible for the story idea—then, because of the way he feels about me, I thought I should be honest and tell him that you'd asked for the date. And of course I told him why you wanted it, and why you asked me—so—

"Oh, Dan, will you *please* take me home!"

He nodded. "Yes, of course. Sure, Mathilda."

They went out into the hall. Someone greeted Dan, and he answered in his usual friendly manner. They went down the stairs, around and down again.

Quite a lot of young people were on the "social floor," and there again Dan exchanged greetings, a word or two. Mathilda touched his arm; he glanced at her, then nodded to his friends. "Can't stop now. I'll be back pretty soon, I'm afraid."

To the laughter, they went outside and to his car. Here the lights were bright, and there was a patrol. Dan explained the need for protection as he put her into the seat, went around to his own, and pulled away from the curb. Mathilda paid no attention. She was thinking.

"Dan," she broke in, "will you tell me how you used that little incident I told you, about the man with the abscessed tooth—how did you build that into a book? I know I didn't tell you more."

"No, you didn't," he agreed. "But I asked around, the way I know how to do. I got some other details—there was a doctor, an older man—who talked about the case to me."

Mathilda groaned. Dr. Alexander. He was another one who talked too much. And of course he knew about Mr. Sherwin. Had Dr. Alexander connected himself with the case?

"I built up the story," Dan was saying, "and selected, then developed the characters."

39

"What characters, and what story?" Mathilda asked. "That a man had an abscessed tooth?"

He laughed. "Of course not! That became just a motivating incident."

Whatever that meant. Mathilda's busy mind was going off in a dozen directions. She could dredge up a dozen happenings that she would think might become "incidents" from which to develop a story.

Take Mrs. Bailey, the patient today on whom they could not proceed and operate. Mathilda could just imagine what misery that poor woman and her husband would be in right then. The shock, the disappointment, the fear with which they would meet future decisions. They could disagree . . . Their families could oppose . . . It always took a lot of courage to face open heart surgery, trust in one's doctor being a prime factor. So one could write a story about *that* relationship.

Dan was joggling her shoulder. "Hey, you!" he cried. "You're home. And I'm afraid to ask if I can come up."

"Oh, yes," she said, retrieving her purse, which had slipped from her lap. "I was wondering about how you could build a book, what characters you used, and all."

Gently, he helped her out of the car, bent and kissed her cheek. "You're tired," he said.

She looked up at him. "I do thank you for the dinner," she told him, "but I wish I'd never heard of your book."

"I am glad I wrote it, Mathilda, and proud. I've always wanted to be proud of something I did."

She nodded. "But you won't tell me any more about what you put into the book?"

He laughed and opened the apartment door for her.

40

"I'm afraid you'll have to read it to find that out," he said gaily.

Mathilda gazed at him. "You sound pretty high," she said dryly.

"Six feet off the ground," he agreed. "Good night, sweetheart."

She nodded. "Good night."

Chapter Three

As she could have expected, and probably did, Mathilda worried throughout the night. She took a warm bath and tried to fasten her mind on anything, everything, other than the evening which she had spent. She refused, absolutely, to think forward to Dan's interview with Mr. Fichter. And then she spent thirty restless minutes speculating upon what would be said during that interview. She progressed to the point of wondering if, just possibly, she could talk to Karen Butler about the THING.

Karen was her close friend; she would judge Mathilda's story fairly. She was one of the assistant administrators of the hospital complex. In fact, unless something intervened, tomorrow morning, Mathilda would be escorting Karen through the cardiac surgical department on one of her routine and regular surveys. Of course Mathilda couldn't talk about personal things then, but she could set up a means—or time—She could even call Karen tonight. She looked at the clock. Sure. Karen would welcome a past-midnight chat about Dan Kearnes's blasted book!

Though it was important, or the Administrator himself would not have asked Dan to come in.

Dan's situation was out of Mathilda's hands, but her own might need a little work on it.

Maybe she'd do better not to tell anyone of her involvement. Dan had promised he would not mention her name. If she had not already told Brook—no one else would know. She wished she had not told Brook.

She wished she could go to sleep!

She punched her pillow. She got up, slim and small-looking in her blue pajamas, and put milk into a saucepan, heated it. She stood drinking it, hating hot milk, but she had to do something!

Tomorrow was a work day, surgery or not, and she could not face it jittery from a sleepless night, dopey for want of sleep.

She went back to bed and tried to make herself relax. "Begin with the top of your head," she advised herself, "eyes, cheek muscles, mouth, chin . . ." She shivered. She bounced out of bed, turned off the air conditioner and opened a window. The noise of the street came up to her, though traffic was light at that hour. But there was traffic —a siren and howler marked the progress of an ambulance going to the hospital three blocks away. She looked down into the street. Under the light at the corner, two women waited for a bus.

"I'm glad I don't have to be out there alone at this hour," said Mathilda half aloud.

The air coming in through the open window was hot and humid. Heat lightning flared along the horizon. Tomorrow would be another hot day. She closed the window, turned on the air conditioner and lay down.

Okay. She couldn't sleep. So what? She would think about tomorrow. The alarm would go off at six-thirty—not that it would be needed. She'd take a quick shower, dress, drink some orange juice, eat a piece of toast and drink some coffee. Midmorning she would get a Danish.

Before leaving the apartment, she would wash the dishes, straighten and close the couch bed, and make a grocery list of things she would buy as she came home tomorrow evening. Toothpaste, bread, a can of fruit— lettuce . . .

What time was Dan's interview with Fichter? Had he told her the time? Did it matter?

Of course it mattered! Mathilda couldn't be anywhere near the business offices, but she would want to *know!*

She hoped Dan would not be "high" the next morning. She hoped he would dress soberly, and act—well—naturally. This would be no time for cuteness.

During the hours remaining she did sleep, fitfully, waking and dozing, not resting to any needed degree.

When she made her couch-bed the next morning, she thought wryly of the night she had spent. "Looks like Barney Google *and* his horse had slept here . . ." She laughed. That was a saying her mother often used about a torn-up bed. Well—

Miss Butler joined Miss Roberts at eight the next morning. Miss Butler was a tall, dark-haired young woman, ten years older than Mathilda, but the two had become good friends, through the assistant administrator's admission that, while she could become excited about the purchase of a new trash compactor or a water retractor in the laundry, the love of her life was the operating rooms.

That morning she came up on Surgical and asked if one of the doctors meant to accompany them. One usually did, said Mathilda.

"Dr. Solley, by choice?"

Mathilda managed a faint grin. "I haven't seen him this morning," she said.

"You look a little peaked, don't you?"

The nurse felt of her starched cap. "I work too hard. I—"

"Are you girls ready?" said a voice behind them.

They whirled. They definitely were not ready. But Dr. Damery was—long white coat, bow tie and chartboard.

"Be right with you, Chief," said Miss Butler, following Mathilda, who already was putting on the surgical gown which was the uniform for the inspection of the area.

Dr. Damery stood out in the hall, smiling at the flurry he had stirred. His eyes were on the windows of ICU; they would visit Intensive Care later.

Dr. Damery was a big man who did not look big. His face was pleasant rather than handsome, his keen blue eyes were capable of seeing everything at once. Over them he wore large, round-lensed glasses, wire-framed. He was head of the Department of Thoracic and Cardiac Surgery, and he brought repute and fame to all of St. Jerome's. Besides this, he was popular. Everyone seemed to like Dr. Damery.

"I wonder if he has his white gloves," said Butler, tying Roberts' gown, then turning to have her own adjusted and made secure.

Mathilda pulled a gauze cap over her red-brown locks and opened the door. Dr. Damery had been known to wipe his gloved fingers along the pipes up against the ceiling of o.r.

In charge of housekeeping at the hospitals, it was Karen

45

Butler's job to keep ahead of people like Dr. Damery. She usually did, too, because she was as convinced as he that in surgery one had the epitome of what a hospital was supposed to be. She recognized the drama that was present, but she stressed the absolute coordination and teamwork of everyone surgically involved in helping the patient.

Their inspection was meticulous and thorough. From floor tile to ceiling pipe, from autoclave to instrument cabinet, everything fell under Miss Butler's eye. The whole surgical floor was looked at, scrubrooms, Recovery and ICU, the o.r.'s, the supply closets and the cleaning utensils.

Halfway through, busy with her own chartboard, Mathilda had a thought. It startled her, and threatened to distract her, which was not good. Such items as needed attention must be noted and later corrected.

But she was thinking, too, that Karen's demanding job required her, on every seventh week, to stay at the hospital, to sleep in the interns' dormitory, ready to be the first one to know about any malfunction in the system, whether it was a leaky air conditioner, muffins not showing up on a patient's breakfast tray, or wrinkles in the lobby carpeting.

On one of these occasions a phone call had shattered Karen's sleep. She had told Mathilda about that call; an adult patient, male, wearing only a hospital gown, was wandering about the grounds, which were too close to the street for complete privacy or even decency.

Mathilda dropped her pencil, and Dr. Damery stooped to retrieve it. "I'm sorry," she murmured, her cheeks red.

But that patient had been the same man who had had the abscessed tooth. Had Mathilda told Dan Kearnes about it? Had he put that incident also into his book? Had he . . . ?

She glanced up at the clock.

She did *wish* she knew when Dan would be seeing Mr. Fichter. Maybe Karen would know. Mathilda gave herself a shake. She wouldn't know, and if she did, she would not say! Today Karen's job was to inspect, and Mathilda's was to conduct her through the surgical area, to make notes and answer questions, not to ask them. Miss Butler, now discussing a light situation in O.R. 2 with Dr. Damery, was not about to fret over Mathilda's worries and concerns.

Mathilda should keep still about Dan Kearnes and his book, and remember again that if Karen, working out of the administrative offices, knew of the appointment with Mr. Fichter, she would have no information or comment to pass on to Mathilda.

If she knew, she wouldn't say. Only Mathilda Roberts talked—which she should not do!

And that determined—Dr. Damery having hurried off about other matters—when Mathilda and Karen were going back to get rid of their baggy surgical gowns. Mathilda was astounded to hear herself telling Karen all about Mrs. Bailey. About what had happened, and not happened, to that poor woman, and, besides that, recounting all the worried imaginings she had entertained on the subject.

She heard her voice, she saw the gestures she made, she saw Karen listening, and she broke off abruptly.

47

"What's wrong?" Karen asked, handing Mathilda the gown. "You look—funny."

"I don't feel funny," said Mathilda crossly. "I feel sunk. I feel terrible."

"Why? Nothing turned up this morning. Both Dr. D. and I were pleased."

"Oh, sure. I can sub for the Supervisor and keep Surgical going. But there is one thing I simply cannot do, Karen, and that is to stop talking so much. I rattle on and on, and I have to learn to keep still."

Karen smiled at her. "We enjoy your chatter. You mean no harm, Mathilda."

"I mean no harm, but I should not talk so much. And I won't, in the future."

Karen laughed. "Be sure your nameplate is on so we'll know you. I have to run, sweetie. How about a movie some evening?"

Mathilda nodded. "Sure," she said gloomily.

"I'll call you."

Karen went elsewhere. Mathilda busied herself with her usual tasks, adding to them her report on the inspection and the items listed for change, requisition, discard. The Supe would want that exactly right! She must inventory the o.r.'s.

It was almost eleven when Brook stuck his head around the door. "Have you had your break?" he asked.

Mathilda looked up from her chartboard, frowning. She had seen Brook twice during the inspection. He'd been making rounds and supervising some dressings . . .

Now he laughed at her blank face. "Remember me?" he asked.

48

She smiled too, and came toward him. "I wish the Supe would do the inspections," she said.

"I imagine you do them better. Damery thinks you do."

"Well, I don't argue. But that's because I'm scared to. Not with anyone from Administration and certainly not with the Chief."

"He doesn't bite. How about coffee?"

"Oh, yes, sure. I'm starved, too."

"You're always starved."

Having located themselves at the desk, they went down to the building cafeteria and found a table against the wall. Some personnel were already getting their lunches, but the place was not crowded or noisy, as it was when filled with people.

Mathilda stirred her coffee and broke off a piece of her hazelnut "claw." "Brook," she asked, "why do I talk so much?"

He leaned back in his chair and regarded her. "What have you done now?" he asked quietly.

"Oh—nothing, I hope. But this morning I found myself telling Karen all about Mrs. Bailey."

Brook nodded. "She's doing very well. She is somewhat discouraged, but I feel sure she will be all right."

"I looked at her chart."

"Yes. And I don't really think, Tillie, that you need worry over telling Karen about that case. The whole hospital is talking about it."

Mathilda ate the piece of Danish. "Yes," she agreed. "But after what you said to me yesterday—What makes me *do* that, Brook? Talk so much, I mean. I know I shouldn't."

He watched her, a faint smile growing in his eyes. "The reason you do it, dear, is your warm heart. You let yourself get personally involved with the patients. With all the patients. Their troubles become your troubles, and if you have a trouble—being you—you tell others about it. So—because you are in close touch with many patients, you talk too much."

She nodded. "I don't think I'd be very good at considering patients as room numbers. Some of the nurses do that."

"And some of the doctors, too. No, you wouldn't be good at it. But since you asked me why you—"

"Why I talked too much. And you said I was soft-hearted and soft-headed."

He laughed aloud. "I didn't say any such thing! I said you let yourself get involved. And you do, Tillie! Do you remember that little boy in the wheelchair? We passed him as we came down here."

Mathilda nodded. "Yes. He was such a little tyke, and so frightened at everything. I hope nothing is really wrong with him."

Brook put his big hand warmly over hers. "Eat your Danish," he said. "But that's what I want to point out to you. You immediately let yourself become involved with *him*. He's here for tests, evidently, from the papers hung on his chair. Probably some small thing brought him here. He was small, and his eyes were big, but kids are tough, and anyway, you can't take them all on your mind, Tillie. You just can't."

"I know. So maybe I shouldn't be a nurse."

"That's crazy. How else would I have got to know you? Now, let me fill your cup, and then you can tell me all about your date with Dan Kearnes. That's what I brought you down here for."

He was gone, and back again. "Now," he said, "let's have it."

She laughed. "In the first place, it was not a *date!*"

"Did you have that half-bottle of wine?"

She giggled. "More like a whole one."

"Then it was a date."

"Oh, Brook!"

"All right. Tell me about it. But Kearnes does too like you."

"Well, I hope so. But—well, anyway, we went to that Italian restaurant where Dr. Damery took us last winter."

Brook whistled.

"Yes! And we had antipasto again. Remember how good it was? And I had scampi, but I don't think they agreed with me. I didn't sleep at all well last night. And we danced a little. He's not anywhere near as good a dancer as you are, Doctor."

"Few people are," he said smugly.

Mathilda laughed. "Few people are as immodest about it, too," she said. "Then we went to his apartment."

"*His* apartment?"

"Oh, hush. He just wanted to show me his contract and the check he got."

"He could have put 'em in his coat pocket and shown them to you between the antipasto and the scampi."

Mathilda nodded. "But he didn't."

51

"And for no good reason, I'll bet."

"Oh, Brook!" She decided not to describe the swinging-singles apartment. Perhaps Dan had had no good reason to take her there. But the phone call had squashed all that.

"He knows you're soft-hearted," Brook was saying.

"And soft-headed to match?"

"That, too," he agreed, much too readily. "Tell me about his wonderful book."

Mathilda put her chin on her fist and smiled at Brook. "Could you be a little jealous, Doctor?" she asked.

"Sure I'm jealous. Don't you want me to be?"

"Well, yes, I suppose I do. Only, with Dan . . ."

"The *book!* We'll be late if you talk about Dan."

She nodded. "All right, then, the book. Right now—right last night—it was a stack of typewritten paper. But he did have the contract, and the promise that he would let the publisher see the next two books he will write . . ."

"When?"

"Oh, I don't know *when.* I don't know how long it took to write this one."

"So tell me about it."

She did. It had a medical scene, or background, she said. "Because of his work in hospitals, you know." She said he wouldn't tell her the story. "He says I'll find out when I buy the book."

"Fair enough. If his friends don't buy it, who will?"

"He may even give me a copy. Because he says he's grateful to me."

"You gave him the story."

"No. He says I told him a small incident, what he calls

52

a bare bone, and he used that in building the story and the characters and the scene. The whole book, I suppose."

Brook nodded. "Bones," he said dryly. He lifted his head to listen to the enunciator. He spoke to an intern who passed their table.

"And then," said Mathilda, "the Administrator—Mr. Fichter, you know? He called."

Brook choked on the mouthful of coffee he had just taken. He coughed, and swore a little, and wiped his mouth and his eyes, and coughed some more. "Go on," he said to Mathilda, "tell me what the—Administrator— wanted with Dan Kearnes. What time was this?"

He was still strangling, but would be all right, Mathilda decided. So, chattering, talking fast, gesturing, she told about the call and the appointment. "Dan was pretty upset," she said, "and I just didn't understand it at all. I spent a lot of time wondering what I had told him that he could use in a story that could upset Mr. Fichter. You see, Dan told me how the publisher checked on names of doctors here in the city, and then he said he supposed they were checking on the story line—he called it that. I wouldn't know about such things for myself—and he seemed pretty upset."

"But he didn't tell you what the story line was."

"No, he didn't. But he did seem frightened—well, not *frightened*—but—well, I don't know the exact word. He was bothered, and some worried—and I got worried, too, in case I *had* told him some small incident that he'd used, one that would upset Mr. Fichter."

"Was he upset?"

"Oh—I don't really know, Brook. He called, and that

53

in itself seemed strange. It was about ten o'clock." Her eyes lifted to his face.

"Yes, it was strange."

"I thought so. And he asked Dan to come to see him today, but I never did know just what time."

"Why didn't you ask him?"

"I didn't think of it. Until he took me home."

"Good! I wasn't sure he had."

"You know I can kick you under this small table."

"I know you'd better not."

"I guess so. You being a senior resident, and all."

He leaned across and pulled a lock of her hair. Hard. She yelped, and he told her to be quiet.

"But you . . ."

"Tell me about Fichter and why he scared the pants off you."

"Brook *Solley!*"

He laughed and settled back into his chair. "I'm sorry. I can't say things like that until after we're married, can I?"

"If we ever are."

"We shall be. Better tell me, Tillie. And I love you anyway."

She knew that her face was getting pink. Brook said she was the only nurse in the hospital who still could blush.

"Dan talked a little about why Fichter wanted to see him, but he didn't know himself, so of course I got very little from him. I kept thinking and thinking and—and around four this morning I decided that he'd made his story around how Fichter got his job. If that was told to the Administrator by the publisher, he would certainly want to squash some of it, wouldn't he?"

"Was that why he called Kearnes? To squash the story?"

"I don't know. I believe Dan thought it was. And if he told how Fichter maneuvered— He really did, Brook. You know he did! He knocked down everyone who had applied, and some of them seemed pretty well qualified. There was that radiologist—Peoples. He really wanted the place. I was in training, but Fichter even talked to us. Then they made a hospital attorney acting manager, and Fichter got *him* to resign."

"How'd he do that?"

"Oh, I don't know. He just did. Maybe Dan tells how in his book."

Brook's eyebrows went up.

"And there were a couple of others. That ex-army man —"

"But he did serve as Acting for nearly a year."

"I know he did. Then Mr. Fichter showed that he was spending above budget. He thought that would get him the job. At that time, Mr. Fichter was in accounting, wasn't he?"

"I wouldn't be surprised."

Brook was being aggravating, but she swept on with her thesis. "I don't recall just how the preacher came into the picture."

"Preachers are supposed to be honest."

"But they don't know much about hospital administration. Anyway, *he* didn't last, and finally Mr. Fichter got the job. He told some gossipy stories about the preacher's wife, I think."

Brook was gazing at the clock.

"I suppose Mr. Fichter is doing a good job . . ."

"He is."

"But he wouldn't want a book written about how he got that job. I imagine he would be furious."

"Was he furious when he called Kearnes?"

"Oh, I don't know, Brook. I heard only Dan's side of the conversation. He just kept saying 'Yes, sir.' 'No, sir.' But he was shook, I could tell. And when he put down the phone, he fixed himself a stiff drink."

The bitch box crackled and called out a message. A bell rang. And more people were coming into the room. At a table over in the corner there was a loud burst of laughter.

Brook was sitting thoughtful. "Am I talking too much again?" Mathilda asked him anxiously.

"Maybe. But with me it won't hurt."

"But, Brook—" She broke off, her eyes wide. "I haven't told anyone else," she gasped. "About Dan's book, or the date, or—"

"You know we have just so much time down here. This afternoon we have to set up two o.r.'s and do the run-through."

"Yes," she said softly. "I do know."

He drained his coffee cup. "I wish one of the procedures could be for Mrs. Bailey," he said briskly. "I'd like to get that one done right away. I am confident the trouble lay with the anaesthesia. It was given too fast, or was the wrong kind for her. I haven't entirely sold Damery on that yet, but I mean to study the situation and try the surgery again. After I've persuaded him, of course. That will take some time, too. You see . . ."

56

He talked for five minutes, which was a lot of talking for Brook.

Mathilda sat back and listened, and watched him.

"You're changing the subject, aren't you?" she asked when he finally gave her a chance. "You're angry."

His eyes flashed blue and green sparks. "What difference does that make?" he demanded. "With you? I was angry yesterday, and you knew it, but you still dated that kook!"

"He's not a kook!" Mathilda cried. "He's just a nice guy . . ."

Brook snorted.

"Well, he is! And I did know you objected to my having dinner with him, but last night—I did know you were angry, but I thought you were heated up because you were jealous."

"I was jealous! Damn right. I love you—I've told you that a dozen times—and you won't marry me, for some silly reason—"

"It's not a silly reason."

"All right. You still owe the bank some money. I could pay that off, and you know I would pay it off. I get a pretty fair salary, and I don't spend much of it, living here at the hospital, and all. So your reason is silly. Unless you resent the fact that I haven't written a book for you to get all excited and starry-eyed about!"

Mathilda laughed. "Oh, Brook!" she cried. She had never known him to act so—so *human,* or talk in such a way. "You have much more going for you than Dan Kearnes does. You're going on staff in a month or two, and everyone thinks Damery is taking you into his office."

"Has he told you that?"

"No, of course not. But I'm sure he's talked to you. Besides, you could write a book if you wanted to. There's plenty of material around here. You must know a hundred blockbuster stories!"

"You don't think much of ethics, do you?" he asked coldly.

He stood up and held his hand out to her. She had been ready to speak, but she said nothing as they threaded their way out of the room. She was thinking—ethics did not feature necessarily in the stories Brook, or she, could tell. Stories of sacrifice, of triumph, defeat—her mind spun off in a dozen directions.

Brook held the door for her, and she ducked under his arm. They started down the hall. "Your book's story," he said, "is not what you think, Tillie. It's not about the Administrator and his job. Though, I suppose, that would make a book. There was a lot of fascinating management went on then. But . . ."

She caught at his arm. "Are you telling me . . . ?" she demanded. "Do *you* know what Dan's book is about?"

"Why shouldn't I know? I'd say, by now, that half the hospital knows."

She began to shake. That abscessed tooth, and— "I don't know," she said stiffly. "I haven't heard what half the hospital has heard. I've spent the morning with Miss Butler and Dr. Damery, and they did not tell me. And *you* have just let me sit and babble for twenty minutes." She was stiff with hurt that Brook should treat her so. She tried to walk away from him, but there was only one way to go, and of course he kept up with her.

58

"I like to hear you babble," he said. "Karen and Damery wouldn't have heard the story, perhaps. And they certainly would not have discussed it if they had. In that case, they, like others, would suppose you knew all the facts, the way you go on dates with Kearnes, and—"

"Oh, stop it!"

He smiled at her and waited for her to enter the elevator. "We have to be finding the tenth floor," he reminded her.

"I'll go straight up to twelve," she said stiffly.

"Good! I'll go with you." He pushed another button.

"Kearnes's book," he said softly, "is about the Sherwin case." He was watching her alertly, the way he watched a patient.

The Sherwin case. Her spirits sank. Yes. She had mentioned the abscessed tooth. She tried to remember how Dan had reacted. But, in any case, she *had* told him about that.

And she felt terrible. She really did.

She went cold, she went hot, and then she felt cold and faint again. Brook put his hand strongly on her arm and led her out of the elevator. She supposed her face had gone every color, that guilt showed all over her. He was letting her work her own way through realization of what all this meant. They walked slowly along the hall toward the desk.

Before they reached it, she turned to face him. "But that all happened two years ago!" she gasped. "I was in training when it began, and barely out of it when . . ."

He nodded. "That's right," he agreed. "I had just gone in here as chief surgical resident in Thoracic. You were a

59

redheaded kid we weren't sure could stand up to open hearts and lungs and pumps and things."

"I have! I do."

"Yes. Of course you do."

She was very upset and afraid she would cry. She snatched her cap from her head. "I'm going to set up," she told him over her shoulder.

He stood watching her. She glanced back at him. "Will there be a briefing?"

"Oh, yes. Around three. You know what we have? There are two cases."

"Yes," she said. He was concerned. He knew, she knew, that the surgical schedules were available. She knew they had a lung and heart patch. The second case was a valve replacement on a teen-ager.

"I'll do rounds," said Brook, looking very tall and stern in his white garments. "Then I'll be in my office. I have paper work up to here." His hand indicated his eyebrows.

"Yes, Doctor," she murmured, and turned into scrub.

In an hour, still wearing the mop-cover cap and the shapeless gown, she knocked softly, then opened his office door and slipped inside. Her face was still white and sober, her hazel eyes as round as coasters.

"Are you ready for me so soon?" he asked.

"Oh, no! But I had to talk to you! I've been thinking—"

He reached his hand and indicated the chair beside his desk. His office was small, hospital space being at a premium. The walls were lined with shelves, and they

60

were crowded with books, journals and folders. A fresh white coat hung on the clothes tree. Brook poured cold lemonade from a thermos and handed the paper cup to Mathilda. "You look sunk," he said. "I am sorry."

"I'll be all right. I— You asked if I was ready. The o.r.'s are. I really hustled the crew."

"You must have."

"I did. Because I wanted a chance to talk to you some more."

He leaned back in his chair, sipped at his own cup. "You didn't get lunch?"

"I'd had that Danish. We often miss lunch up here. How's Mrs. Bailey?"

"Oh, she's fine. Doing just fine!"

"That's good. Well—I'm glad you told me that it is the Sherwin case Dan used. I don't like to get sunk before strangers."

"You took it pretty well, all things considered."

She managed a weak smile, and he patted her forearm. "All things, including a malpractice suit," she agreed.

"There never was one. It was hushed up."

Mathilda nodded. "Yes, but I never knew just how they managed to do that."

"It would seem that Dan Kearnes knew. Or found out."

Mathilda gulped. "The book," she said gloomily. "Do you suppose that is what he used? Well, of course it was, or Fichter wouldn't have been upset. Oh, Brook, this is terrible, isn't it?"

"Yes, it could be."

Her face brightened. "But if I don't know how that

61

hush-up was arranged, how could I have had a thing to do"—her voice trailed away—"with any of it?" she concluded faintly.

"You must have said *something*, Tillie, to start him . . ."

"Well, anybody could have said *something!*" she cried.

"Yes, they could have. Except that he told you, and took you to dinner, because he says you helped him."

Mathilda sat shaking her head. "Not about the malpractice suit," she said. "I couldn't. I do remember . . . Oh, I've been thinking so *hard*, Brook!"

Her face was pinched, and he laughed gently. "It shows," he said kindly.

"I suppose it does. I don't do nearly enough of it. But, Brook, I'm sure that the only thing I ever told Dan about the Sherwin case was that—and I didn't say much—but I did talk a little about the old doctor. I can't even remember his name."

"Alexander."

"Yes, that's what it was. He was a heart specialist."

"Of a sort," Brook agreed. "And if that is all you talked about—"

"And the abscessed tooth," said Mathilda in a small voice.

"You talked about *that?*"

"I think so. I said the old doctor brought the man in as a heart case when the real trouble was an abscessed tooth."

"Oh, *Tillie!*" Brook got out of his chair. There was not much room to pace, but he made the most of it—and filled all of it. Mathilda watched him, her face white again. If

62

Brook was really mad at her—

"That would do it!" he exclaimed. "He probably asked a question or two—"

"I didn't tell him another thing!"

"You're positive? Though he probably did ask other people. He's a trained reporter."

Yes, Dan had said he'd asked around. Mentioning her? Mathilda shivered and buried her face in the paper cup of lemonade. "The Sherwin case," she said into its depths. "The Sherwin case."

Chapter Four

THE Sherwin case.
The Sherwins.

An ultra-conservative family that had incredibly become entangled with the affairs of as big and diverse a project as St. Jerome's Hospital Center.

Not a doctor in the Sherwin family itself, not people ever to feature in newspaper items, they lived respectable, well-controlled lives. They deplored publicity or any other disruption of their dignity. They . . .

There was Mark Sherwin, a well-known man in the city and in the suburban areas west of the city, well known in banks, at the Noonday Club, at the country club.

There was Victoria, his wife, friendly, gregarious, in her own circles, and among people, to quote her, "who could be trusted."

There was Peter Sherwin, the only son, now approaching forty, a lawyer who cherished his position in life and that of his family. He had attended the best schools, country day, then the stuffiest prep school available, and a university to match. He had graduated from Harvard Law. He joined one of the best conservative law firms in his native city, and was persuaded to run for a minor judgeship to which he was handily elected. His father called him Judge Sherwin; few others did except in professional circles.

Rich. Respectable. The Sherwins felt secure in those categories. They liked what life had given them, and expected to enjoy its gifts.

There was Helen Sherwin, a friendly woman in her mid-thirties. A lady, by sight and behavior. Clothes, hair, manner, always correct, always admired. Cool, untouchable, gracious.

And there was Helen Sherwin's father.

He was, he had been, a physician well thought of in the town where he had been born, grown up, and practiced medicine for fifty years. Like many doctors of his generation, he was a general practitioner, a family physician. As retirement age loomed, he decided to limit his practice to heart patients. In this new capacity, he traveled extensively to meetings of heart and chest doctors, attended lectures and received certificates which were framed and hung on his office walls.

The town where he lived was a small city of 25,000 people. It was three hundred miles from the big city, from St. Jerome's, from the Sherwins.

But by his nature and activities, he became involved in the Sherwin case. He involved himself.

Mark Sherwin, the lead in the drama, was a tall, handsome man. He had begun his adult life as a contractor, and along the way had built, or acquired, a large list of properties. Now, retired from the building of condominiums, hotels, and apartment complexes, he supervised those he owned, and he owned enough to qualify himself as a very

65

rich man. He was convivial and popular, a good talker, well liked.

Victoria, his wife, had enjoyed her life, too. The daughter of a socially established family, she was a tall, lean woman; her face was on the horsy side, but she looked very well in tweeds and tailored linens. She filled her life with club meetings, bridge and golf. She regularly took trips—to Arizona in the winter, Colorado and Lake Placid in the summer. Sometimes Mark went with her, more often he did not. He liked his home, and preferred to stay there.

Their union had been blessed with one child, a son, whom they had cherished and nurtured very close to the point of dependency. Peter Sherwin was not a handsome man; his brown hair was straight and thin; he wore thick-lensed glasses, and besides being the spoiled son of a rich man, he was afraid of everything. He lived with fear—of assignment to crime court, of physical hurt and pain. He would not stay in a hotel room above the sixth floor, his own home was guarded by every automatic electric device, none of which he really trusted. He survived on yogurt, blackstrap, wheat germ and granola. He mistrusted restaurant food. He ate fertile eggs until his father-in-law instructed him on the dangers of cholesterol. Then he would not have eggs, or bacon, in his home. Mark and Victoria tolerated his notions, but were famed, and popular, for the lavish food at the parties they gave. Peter, they told themselves, their friends, and each other, was a fine lawyer.

And they were genuinely fond of the girl whom Peter had married. Both had attended eastern universities—

66

Helen's was not coeducational, and neither was Peter's, at that time. They had met at some prom weekend, had extended the friendship, and then the courtship. Like Peter, Helen had led a sheltered childhood and life. As a wife, with her own home, she became the perhaps typical Junior League type of young woman; one saw her prototype on the golf links of any fine country club. Helen did charity work and ran her beautiful home well. She had taste and good manners. She was especially active in church work, and she paid regular visits to her parents. They, in turn, came to see her. Helen's life was full.

She was a slender woman with a pleasant, not pretty, face. Her hair was dark blonde, and, according to the current style, was worn only slightly waved, and long to her shoulders. She wore little jewelry, her clothes were always exactly right, becoming to her, and suitable to the occasion.

The Peter Sherwins' best friend, perhaps, was a bachelor doctor who once had lived in one of the Sherwin apartments. Peter and Helen had lived across the hall from him for the years it took them to decide on, and build, their own home. As he became busier and household tasks too burdensome, the doctor had moved to a hotel. But the three remained friends, enjoyed the theater together, and had season tickets for the same seats each year, just as they sat together for the symphony concerts on Friday nights. They played bridge together, and for a time belonged to a duplicate group.

Helen and Peter, jointly and separately, had tried to find a wife for the doctor; he had resisted all their efforts, amused, but not ready to capitulate. He was perhaps five

67

years older than Peter, and seven or eight years older than Helen. The three were close friends, each enjoying the friendship, and not inclined to violate the other's privacy.

Gordon Damery was good company in every situation, but he also was a surgeon, serious about his work. He had trained, studied and worked until he was considered to be one of the five finest heart surgeons in the country. He had brought prestige to the city and to the St. Jerome's medical complex. He was not a handsome man; his face was on the heavy side, deeply lined about his mouth. His blue eyes were keen; he wore round-lensed spectacles. He spoke in a soft voice, and quickly. He was intense in all that he did, and would gesture with his pink, soft hands, wagging his long forefinger when he talked. He read widely, and had a colossal memory. He had early passed the Boards, and had served on the staff of several hospitals. He became Chief of Thoracic Surgery at St. Jerome's five years after he came to know the Peter Sherwins. Finally, he took over the tremendous task of serving as Chief of the big hospital's surgical service. He was pleasant but firm, devoted to his work, understanding but seldom forgiving of failure in those who worked with him. He had built up a reputation for himself, and for the hospital, and cherished that reputation jealously.

Dr. Hubert Alexander bragged about his acquaintance with Dr. Damery and was not above letting people think he worked with the famous man. He had indeed met Dr. Damery a few times at the Christmas Eve buffets which always were held at the Mark Sherwin home. The old doctor and his Dresden-doll wife Margaret always spent Christmas with Helen and Peter. Of course they were invited to the Mark Sherwin buffet, and occasionally Dr. Damery could be persuaded to attend. Except that he was Helen's father, it was doubtful if Damery remembered the thin, fuss-budget Dr. Alexander. Dr. Damery fervently disliked talking surgical shop at parties. Dr. Alexander knew how to talk little else.

When he went home, or anywhere, from these few brief contacts, he built up a close relationship and told about seeing "my friend, Dr. Gordon Damery." He told about meeting other friends of the Sherwins too, but "knowing" Dr. Damery was the star in his crown. He talked and talked about it.

It became his practice, when he went to the city to visit Helen and Peter, always to go to St. Jerome's. Museums, the theater, and certainly the symphony, had absolutely no appeal for Dr. Alexander. "All my life's been doctoring," he would assert, and proudly. "I don't know anything about anything else."

This was true enough. Retirement was very difficult for the former family doctor. He had no hobbies, no other skills. So, when he traveled, he visited hospitals. When he went to visit his daughter, he went to St. Jerome's. Helen had asked Gordon Damery if he might.

"Well, of course, dear. I'll give him a guide if he wants."

"I just think he wants to play firehorse and sniff smoke."

Dr. Damery said the proper words, and Dr. Alexander was in heaven. Everyone was courteous to him, now and then someone would spare a few minutes to talk to him. He visited the whole complex, getting a map and designing activities for each day he would be in the city. But he

69

always gave some time to the thoracic surgery floors. Once he was allowed to observe Dr. Damery in surgery, and came out of that long session like a man dazed. He talked and talked about the experience to anyone who would listen. Back home, a lot of people had the idea that he'd been down on the floor, scrubbed and working, so familiar and experienced did he sound when he told about the procedures of open heart surgery, from the ankle vein-strip to the last skin suture. Heart-lung machine, anaesthesia, the sutures used—he knew it all, and told it all.

It isn't known whether he ever met or spoke to Dr. Damery on these visits. Mainly he just hung around the desks, patrolled the halls, visited with patients' families in the sunrooms, or even with the patients in their rooms. He always wore a long white lab coat when he visited the surgical floors, with his name tag properly in place on his left breast pocket. The personnel found out who he was, and were patient with him if he didn't get in the way, and he didn't, often. He understood the limitations. ICU, o.r. were forbidden territories to a great many people who did have reason for being on Thoracic.

Dr. Alexander liked 13 best, the surgical floor, but he spent most of his time on 12 where the patients were; he made a pattern of visiting in their rooms and with the family members who also visited.

He would explain that he was a retired heart specialist, still "ready to help out if needed."

The hospital personnel heard him say this, and adopted the classification themselves, some derisively, but most out of a wish to be kind to a nice old man. They called him Doc. "I see Doc is back," the floor Head would say to another nurse, her eyes following the slightly stooped, bald-headed man going swiftly along the corridor.

"He's checking on us."

"We'd better pay attention to him. I heard him tell someone in the sunroom that modern doctors neglected their post-op patients."

The second nurse glanced at the monitoring control panel where lights blinked or burned steadily, where pulse, respiration and blood pressure were continuously reported.

"Oh, he knows all about Big Brother," laughed the head nurse. "He thinks the patients need more of the personal touch, the pulse taken by warm fingers on the wrist, a few friendly words spoken, and questions asked."

"You know? He may have something there."

"Yes, he probably does. He says our surgeons don't come near a p.o. once the fellow gets out of ICU."

"But . . ."

"He doesn't think an earnest intern is any substitute."

"Boy, he can get us all in trouble."

"Do you think he really is a heart man?"

"Oh, no. Not practicing, anyway. Of course he talks about heart massage. But I don't think he'd have the strength to open a chest, or even give it a good lick with his fist. He talks about acupuncture, too. Says he wouldn't be afraid to use it."

"Not on me!"

"No. Nor me."

The women laughed and went about their duties. The old gentleman could be something of a nuisance, but on the whole he was treated very well.

Those were the Sherwins, one of their friends, and one of their relatives. It was against this setup that Mark Sherwin had a heart attack—later to be known as "his" heart attack.

It happened on a late evening in summer. Mark Sherwin had put in a full day—first in his office, and lunch with friends at the athletic club in the city. He had then driven —too fast, probably—as was his practice—out to one of the apartment complexes which he had built, and still owned. This was out in the county, and was a popular, always full place. But the management of such a complex demanded constant attention, what with the grounds, the variations in tenants, the problems to be met with work-men—painters, plumbers, carpenters being only a few.

From this place, Mark Sherwin, bronzed from the sum-mer's sun, tired, but wanting a change in that tiredness, drove to the country club, changed his gray silk suit and deep blue shirt to brown slacks and a peach-colored pullover, and went out to the golf course. It was never too difficult to make up a late afternoon foursome at the club, and the three men with whom he played that evening were friends. Each of them had had a drink or two in the locker room, and they planned on dinner together after the game. "If our wives will let us." They enjoyed the game, though it was far from professional golf. There was a lot of laugh-ter and talk.

They had caddies and carts, but from the 18th they decided to walk back to the clubhouse. Maybe someone on the veranda and terrace would think they had walked all the way.

It was a beautiful evening, with the shadows deep and

long across the fairways. Mark was already late for dinner at home, so he decided to call Victoria before he showered.

It was while he was doing this, using the booth in the hall because of the noise in the locker room, that he felt the first grabbing pain in his chest. He blamed it on the ham and cheese omelet which he had eaten for lunch, and he asked the attendant to get him some bicarb. Afterward someone said he had noticed Mark rubbing his arm when he went into the shower.

And it was in the shower, with the water pelting down, that he slumped over, then fell.

This of course created quite an uproar in the shower room. Men shouted and talked excitedly, telling those who came in or out from their own roaring showers what had happened.

One man laughed hysterically and said they made a scene for an X-rated movie, all those naked men!

But no one laughed with him.

Ordinarily there would have been at least one doctor in the clubhouse. That day there was none.

But someone said they needed an ambulance. Someone else asked about putting some clothes on "old Mark." "He looks terrible," he added unnecessarily.

He did look terrible. His face was beaded with perspiration, his color mottled, his eyes anguished. "Feel—awful —" he gasped.

The ambulance came, and the big man was put on a stretcher, then, with difficulty, carried up the narrow stairs and out. Someone said he would phone Peter. Peter could tell Victoria.

Another friend, one of the foursome, offered to go to the

73

hospital with Mark.

The attendant was busy doing the things he had been trained to do for a heart case. This seemed to be one.

They took the stricken man to the County Hospital and into the emergency room, both of which moves upset Peter, who went there at once. He demanded that his father be moved immediately. He said the busy and noisy emergency ward was not for people like Mark Sherwin. He was terrified, and he terrified his father, who knew what had hit him, but since he remained conscious, did not think he was all that bad.

The staff doctor who talked to Peter tried to explain these things—the value of time, of quiet, of complete rest.

Peter would not listen. "Tell me just one thing!" he cried. "Can my father be moved?"

"I wouldn't advise it, Mr. Sherwin."

"That is *not* what I asked!"

The staff doctor shrugged. He was sure he had a coronary. The sooner therapeutic rest was established, the better. But obviously this pigheaded lawyer would listen to nothing he had to say. "I wouldn't advise a move," he said again, and coldly.

"But listen to me! Dr. Damery—of St. Jerome's—I am sure you have heard of him? He is a personal friend. I want him to handle the case!"

"Damery is a surgeon."

"Damery is a heart man!" shouted Peter.

And without Dr. Damery's ever being consulted, Mark Sherwin was taken by another ambulance into the city, to St. Jerome's. He was taken to the Cardiac Center and to the receiving room there. Then Peter tried to reach his

74

friend, Gordon Damery.

"Better let me get in touch with him," said the resident doctor. "If the Chief is in surgery . . ."

"He wouldn't be at this time, would he? It's nine o'-clock!"

The resident smiled at him over his shoulder. "Damery never looks at a clock," he said.

"I want my father to be his patient!"

"Perhaps you would like to wait out in the hall, sir?"

Peter would like to do nothing of the sort, but, surprisingly, he found himself there. He called Victoria, his mother, who had been told by someone at the club about her husband's collapse, though she had earlier talked to Mark, who said he was ill. "He thought he'd eaten some bad ham, dear."

Peter asked her to call Helen. "She could drive you in to St. Jerome's, Mother."

"I could drive in there myself . . ."

"I'd rather you would call Helen and tell her what has happened. Now, Mother, please. I'm busy here."

He was not. He was called to the desk to tell his father's age and say whether he had ever had a heart seizure before. No, he could not go into the receiving room, the doctors were taking good care of Mr. Sherwin.

Yes, Dr. Damery had been told.

And after what seemed hours, Dr. Damery came along the hall, his eyeglasses flashing, a white jacket over his o.r. greens. "What's wrong, Pete?" he asked calmly.

"It's Dad! He's had a heart attack—they won't let me in, so I don't know *how* he is. Would you help us? Please, Gordie?"

75

"Yes, sure." He glanced at the desk. The nurse told him where Mr. Sherwin was. "You wait here," he said to Peter, and he disappeared.

Victoria and Helen arrived before he came out again. He brought another doctor with him whom he introduced as "Dr. Perry. He will take care of your father, who is doing pretty well."

Peter caught at Dr. Damery's arm. "I want *you* to take care of Dad!" he said tensely. "That's why I had him brought here."

Both doctors looked at him sharply. "Brought him from where?" Dr. Damery asked.

"Oh, he had this attack at the club, and they took him to County Hospital. I found him in the emergency room, and of course . . ."

"Where he was getting good care, I am sure," said Dr. Damery crisply. "You took a great risk moving Mark, Peter."

"I wanted *you!*"

"Oh, well, now there is something you should understand." He held out his hand to Victoria and Helen, who had been standing back, waiting fearfully until Peter had talked to the doctors. "I want you all to understand this."

He paused, then he said slowly and firmly, "Mark has had a heart seizure. A spasm. We'll determine the extent of injury as we go along. It seems to be of medium intensity, but anything can happen, either way. I have examined him and consulted with the admitting doctor and with Dr. Perry here. But the case is not to be mine, Peter, and should not be. No surgery seems remotely possible, you will be glad to know. So, while I shall admit him—

I already have—and I shall consult with these men, that's as far as my service could or should go."

They had to be content with that. Peter asked if he might stay at the hospital, have a room near his father.

This was refused. "We haven't the space. Besides, you'd scare the man to death."

Victoria was allowed to see Mark for five minutes after he'd been taken to a bed in Intensive Care and hooked up to the monitors. A more complete history was taken, and then the Sherwins were sent home.

Victoria refused to stay with Peter and Helen. "I need my own bed," she said sturdily.

Having deposited her and then gone on to their own home, Peter called the hospital and asked about his father. For a good hour after that he paced the floor, imagining all that could happen, enlarging on all that had happened earlier that evening. But, finally, exhausted, he consented to go to bed. He even drank the bouillon which Helen brought to him. "You seem calm enough," he told his wife accusingly.

"I'm not, really. I love your father very much, as you know. But I trust Gordie. Besides, I plan to call my father and talk to him."

"Good!" said Peter. "That will be another opinion. I just cannot understand Gordie's refusal to take the case."

"Perhaps my dad can explain that to us."

"Well, I certainly hope so!" He settled down into his pillows. Helen took the bouillon cup away and dimmed the room's lights.

In the kitchen, and then in her own bedroom, she considered the telephone and the clock. She knew her father

77

would be shocked at any delay in notifying him of Mark's attack. She also knew that he was seventy-eight years old and that he went to bed at nine-thirty most evenings.

But, finally, after she had bathed and had put a long, dark robe over her gown, she dialed the number of her father's home, three hundred miles away.

She would have to wait, let the phone ring, and ring again. Her father was the sort of doctor who would not keep a telephone beside his bed. He thought he should be wide awake when talking to a patient. That it meant a very loud bell on the phone in the lower hall did not bother him. His hearing was good, though his wife's was not. He considered the hazards of a hurried trip down the stairs in the middle of the night—Helen considered them. Her mind pictured that trip. The stairs were carpeted in blue, and they made two turns between the second and the first floor. Because once a patient had, in the dark, mistaken the stairway for the bathroom door, had fallen and broken her shoulder, Dr. Alexander kept a baby gate latched across the top of his stairway.

So, having been roused from sleep, having thrust his feet into slippers and fumbled with the gate, he would be making his way down the stairs, his bony old shanks well displayed beneath the tails of the nightshirt he stubbornly wore.

The star-shaped crystal lantern in the stairwell would give him plenty of light.

"Helloooo?"

Helen smiled. It was his familiar voice, his familiar greeting.

As quickly and as quietly as he would permit, what with

78

exclamations, ventured opinions and advice interspersed, she told him what had happened that evening to her father-in-law.

No, she didn't know any technical details. Dr. Damery had not seemed concerned.

No, Dr. Damery would not take the case.

"I'll be there!" said Dr. Alexander.

"Oh, Dad, no!"

"Why should you say 'no'? If Peter's father has had a coronary, I belong right there."

"A Dr. Perry is in charge. He's a heart specialist."

"And what am I? That's the trouble with a man's family. They never have any understanding of the work he does. The man studies and works . . ."

Helen had heard that lecture many times. For all she knew, her father actually was a heart specialist, and tops in his specialty. But he was retired . . . old . . .

He had, all her life, tried to combine his busy general practice with the belief that a doctor should not talk about his cases at home. Helen and her mother had resigned themselves to the fact that they always were the last to know who was sick, and how sick. And their patience was rewarded by this speech about a doctor's family never understanding the demands and labors of his profession.

When he paused for breath, she tried to dissuade the old man from starting for the city in the middle of the night.

"Get your rest and come tomorrow, if you want to," she finally conceded. "We'll be glad to have you, and I know you'll be a comfort to Peter."

Of course it did little good. Dr. Alexander and his wife left home at five in the morning. He brought his own outdated, but trusted, EKG machine, the jackets of four suits on hangers, but no trousers, and he left his front door wide open behind them. During the morning, a neighbor saw this and locked it.

Helen made her parents comfortable in what Peter called the in-law wing of their large home, and the hospital treated Dr. Alexander with every courtesy.

He was not encouraged to use his EKG apparatus, but he was allowed to read Mark Sherwin's charts; he went into the intensive care area with Dr. Perry and was introduced to the resident and to the nurse on duty. He used his own stethoscope, and at home talked knowingly of vital signs and infarcts.

The doctors consulted him and invited him to sit in on staff discussions of Mark's case, along with others that came up at those sessions. They listened to what Dr. Alexander had to say.

This made him feel important, as if he were back at work.

Everything was ultra-ethical, and Dr. Damery made a point of being nice to Helen's father. It was he who took him to lunch in the senior staff dining room, and introduced him as a "visit." Dr. Alexander was to tell about this experience for months to follow.

He also talked about the pacemaker which he decided should be implanted but Dr. Damery said was not indicated. He said, oh, yes, he would specifically look into the matter. But he "looked into it," Dr. Alexander complained to Helen and to Peter, by having an "intern" examine and give tests to Mark Sherwin. The intern was

Brook Solley, senior house resident in thoracic surgery, a young doctor whom Dr. Damery thought was on the way "to top us all."

Dr. Alexander did not share this enthusiasm. Call him resident or intern, the young doctor was still wet behind his ears. Who was he to disagree with Dr. Alexander, who had been saving lives before the young squirt was born!

"I think the old gentleman is peeved," Dr. Solley told his chief.

"I know he is. I just wish he wouldn't voice his peeve all over the place. He talks to everyone, Brook! The family, to other patients, even to the newspapers. I had a reporter ask me why I disapproved of pacemakers."

"But—"

"I know. I do use them. They're fine, and will get better. But Mark Sherwin does not need one. We both know that."

"And we've told him and his family."

"What's our word against Daddy Doc's?" asked Dr. Damery, going down the hall fast. Brook raised an eyebrow. He'd never before seen the Chief that upset.

But in spite of all this—Dr. Alexander's peeve and Peter Sherwin's hovering anxiety—Mark Sherwin recovered. He was discharged from the hospital, sustained on an anticoagulant, and a quinidine-type medication to steady his heartbeat; he was given a recommended diet and urged to remember that he was sixty-seven years old. He was told he could resume his activities, oversee his business interests, play some golf. He socialized, though mildly, and at regular intervals he did remember to go back to let Dr. Perry check on the medicines which were given in

81

large doses and needed to be watched.

He recovered, in spite of himself, as well. From the first he had been a difficult patient, objecting to the tubes inserted, objecting to Intensive Care, and then to the room assigned to him. He disliked the food and the appearance of the nurse. He did not want to stay in bed, and when allowed out of it, one summer evening, after visiting friends had left and the nurses were busy with their bedtime duties, he slipped away, went across the hall to the elevator, downstairs, and got outside without being seen. In his flaring hospital gown, his back as bare as the day he was born, he walked about the grounds, bending over the flower beds, standing by the fountain, watching traffic along the busy boulevard, looking across at the park . . .

He strenuously objected when two orderlies brought a robe and seemed ready to take him inside. He thought the hospital regulations were unreasonable. If he was able to walk along the hall, he was able to walk on the lawn. Indecent exposure? Nonsense! Look at any movie, look at the boys and girls in the park, or going down the street. Mark, in his hospital shirt, was much more decently dressed!

Everyone was glad when he was allowed to go home with his list of suggested restrictions and cautions. He threw the paper into the wastebasket and did his best, as he admitted, to "forget that he'd been sick." Almost at once he tried to do the things he had always done, though he did take his medicines and he did report to Dr. Perry.

He went to his office, he went to his properties; he did not play golf because the autumn rains and then winter prevented. But he did swim at the club, and jogged around the track there. He accepted invitations, talked, drank, laughed about as he had always done. This alone terrified Peter.

Mark said his son wanted to wrap the old man in cotton.

"But, Dad," said Helen, "it's just that he's afraid . . ."

"Sure he's afraid. Peter is afraid of everything. That's why you don't have children. He's afraid to bring a child into this world. He's afraid of eggs and whole milk and a well-marbled steak. He wants a fire escape from a first-floor window, and the next thing we know, he won't shake hands or eat in a restaurant for fear of germs."

"Peter isn't that bad, and you know it."

Mark hugged her shoulders. "I'm sorry, Helen. But he does worry so damn much! What's this latest idea of his? I suspect he is trying to get me out of our big Christmas party."

That, exactly, was what Peter had in mind, and he felt triumphant when he succeeded in persuading his parents to visit the Alexanders that Christmas. Once there, he suggested that his father have a checkup at the local hospital, a neat, efficient institution of which Dr. Alexander once had been a part owner. He still maintained staff privileges, and offered to give both of the elder Sherwins checkups. Victoria refused flatly. Mark agreed, though he laughed at the diet sheets which Dr. Alexander produced.

The old doctor still was talking about pacemakers. "If I had the say," he told his guests as they departed, "I'd make you go where a doctor would give you a pacemaker.

83

It would be like double insurance."

It was his daughter who vetoed the idea. "I think we should trust Dr. Demery," she said firmly.

Since Mark wanted no more of hospitals, and certainly not surgery, he agreed with her. He was doing fine, he asserted. And indeed he seemed to be. Though once at home, he firmly refused to eat Dr. Alexander's recommended unsalted oatmeal and skim milk for breakfast. He wanted bacon and eggs, or waffles. "Or both," he added wickedly.

Things gradually returned to normal in the family. Mark seemed to be doing all right. "He is being more sensible than he wants us to think," Victoria told Peter and Helen. "He takes his medicine, and he goes to see Dr. Perry every six weeks."

Victoria, on her part, resumed her travels, her bridge games, served on the boards she had always favored.

Helen and Peter relaxed.

It was months later, more than a year, when Mark Sherwin developed an abscessed tooth. At first, he told no one about it. Victoria noticed that he was not eating with his usual relish. They attended a dinner, they went out to a restaurant, he refused a nut and brown sugar dessert at home. He didn't put ice into his drinks.

"Your face looks swollen," she said one evening. "I don't think you've gained weight, because it's only your face."

Mark got up and left the room. She was concerned, and watched him. His temper got worse and worse. One morning she found a thermometer on the shelf in his bathroom.

She asked Mark about it. "I thought I might have caught a cold," he growled. "What's wrong with taking my temperature?"

"Nothing, I suppose," said Victoria. "Did you have any fever?"

"Half a degree. It's nothing."

He made no mention of his aching tooth to anyone in the family. Since it was a tooth, and he knew it—cold or hot liquids set it on fire and he couldn't chew on that side of his mouth—the damn thing kept him awake at night! —it probably did not occur to Mark to speak of the matter to Dr. Perry, to Peter's father-in-law, or to any other doctor. After nearly a week, he surrendered and went to the dentist, whom he didn't think it necessary to tell about his heart attack or the medicine he was taking.

After treatment, the tooth came out on Friday. The dentist gave the usual instructions—aspirin for pain, use of an ice bag to reduce swelling—"If you have trouble, come in Monday."

Mark went home and told no one that he'd been to the dentist. Victoria was away for three days on some sort of "cultural trip." A dozen women had gone to New York for a binge of theaters, concerts, and dinners at gourmet restaurants. She would be home on Sunday afternoon.

At noon on Sunday, Mark collapsed.

Peter came to the house after church service. He checked on his father regularly these days, Helen explained, relieved that he did.

He found his father limp in his big chair, a bloody towel

in his hand, his color "like death," said Peter.

He called Helen in from the car, and they debated what should be done.

"I'll telephone to Dad," said Helen after the first moments of panic.

She did call Dr. Alexander, finding him having dinner with friends at a local restaurant. He listened to what his daughter had to tell him, and said some angry words about the tooth extraction. "If he's still on anticoagulants—I suppose you've tried to call his personal heart specialist?" His tone turned acid when he mentioned such a man.

"It's Sunday, Dad . . ."

"Yes, and city specialists go into hiding on weekends. I know. But, Helen, it will take me four—or, I guess, five hours to get to the city."

"Oh, you shouldn't think of coming!"

"Well, of course your mother and I will come. But for now you had better take him to the hospital on an emergency basis. His records are there, and they will surely admit him to the heart ward. Maybe your friend Damery will be somewhere around."

He said that sarcastically, too, and Helen shrugged as she set the phone down. "Dad says he should go straight to the hospital. He hopes Gordie is there."

Mark was too weak and too frightened to protest. Peter and Helen drove him to St. Jerome's, forgetting that they were supposed to meet Victoria at the airport. This became one of the lesser crises of that week.

At the hospital, it developed that Dr. Damery was out of town; Mark's family was told that he had gone to a football game in Chicago.

"You know he's a fan," Helen reminded Peter, who was outraged that the doctor was not available. "They are admitting Mark; he'll be taken care of. This whole building takes care of heart cases."

"Heart and lung—the chest," Peter corrected her in his stuffiest fashion. Helen sighed.

Mark was put to bed, and his records produced. Dr. Perry was also out of town; he probably had sent word to Mr. Sherwin? He had gone to Russia with a group of American doctors—a People to People tour. Mark was too weary to be interested. He said, no, he did not want another doctor in charge of his case, or even giving orders.

It was explained to him that there were six or seven other specialists on the staff. Dr. Perry's assistant was there. So was Dr. Solley, Dr. Damery's senior resident—since the Sherwins seemed to want Dr. Damery, though it must be understood, he was a surgeon.

"Yes, yes, we know!" said Peter petulantly. "All right, put a man on the case, and take care of my father!"

But Mark, the bleeding having been controlled—that had frightened him—pointed out that he was conscious and his own man. He refused to have any tests—"any of your damn tests"—started until the next day. "You say Dr. Damery will be back then."

Again it was explained to him that his was not a surgical case.

"We're friends," said Mark stubbornly.

It was Brook Solley who had to tell the recalcitrant Mr. Sherwin that he must follow orders and have the tests made if he stayed in the hospital.

87

Mark glared at the tall young doctor with the stern face, the steady green eyes, and the furlike cap of dark hair. "When did you say Dr. Damery would be back?"

"He'll be here tomorrow, sir, but . . ."

"Have someone get my clothes. I'm going home."

"It will be against medical advice, sir."

"Your advice, you mean?"

"Yes, sir."

"Any time an intern tells me what I can and cannot do . . ." fumed Mark. "Tell my son I want to see him."

He could not be persuaded. He went home. Yes, he would go to bed. All the rigamarole necessary to get him into the hospital had completely exhausted him.

"And us," murmured Victoria.

That evening, Dr. Alexander arrived, his wife with him, of course. Peter took the old gentleman over to see his father. Dr. Alexander set up the old wooden-boxed EKG machine at his bedside. But Mark would have no part of salt paste and leads. "They'll do it at the hospital—when I go back."

"If they'll have you back," said the affronted Dr. Alexander.

"Why wouldn't they?"

"Because you left AMA."

"Humph! Whatever that means."

"You know what it means."

He told Helen and Peter that he did not like the way Mark looked. "His pulse is thready—he should be in the hospital. What about another one?"

"Gordie will be back late tonight," said Helen.

"How do you know that?

"I asked Dr. Solley before we left. Gordie never stays away long."

"Just long enough to go to a football game!" cried Dr. Alexander spitefully. If the family would name *him* as attending physician—but of course he couldn't *say* that!

The next morning, Helen determined that Dr. Damery had indeed returned. Yes, he would admit her father-in-law. "There seems to have been a bloody foul-up here," he told her.

"There was. You know what Mark is." She told about the abscessed tooth. Dr. Damery whistled and asked the name of the dentist.

Mark returned to the hospital no better for all he had put himself through on Sunday, and immediately the tests were made. Neither Dr. Damery nor Dr. Solley appeared at his bedside, but it was certain that they knew the results of the tests. Dr. Damery called Peter and told him that the white count was down to six hundred.

"I'm sure everything possible is being done, Peter, but your father is in a critical condition. You and Helen should be prepared. Your mother, too, of course."

On Tuesday, Mark Sherwin died.

Reviewing the case at Staff meeting, the cardiac service declared the death to be a rather obvious case of involuntary suicide.

"The dentist feels terrible. But he was not told either of the heart attack or the anticoagulant."

"Does the family accept your diagnosis and recognize the death as suicide?" Dr. Damery asked his senior resident.

"No, sir. They accept leukemia as the official cause of death."

Dr. Damery shook his head. "And probably blame me for not detecting it in time."

Dr. Solley gathered up his papers. "For being a surgeon, sir. That's what they blame you for. As a friend, they thought you could have saved his life."

"I couldn't. But, yes, I am a friend of the family."

"It makes things harder."

"It certainly does."

As a friend of the family, Dr. Damery attended Mark Sherwin's funeral, and was rewarded by a stiff nod from Peter. After the service, Dr. Alexander came up to him, bristling with indignation and injured vanity, stuttering over what he wanted to say to this big-shot specialist.

"Mark Sherwin was a fine man!" he declared truculently.

"Yes, he was," said Dr. Damery. "He died entirely too young."

"But he didn't die of what you wrote down on his certificate!" cried Dr. Alexander, his voice shrill.

Dr. Damery glanced around the narthex of the big church at the well-dressed, and curious, people waiting to go out to their cars.

"There is always room for disagreement in these cases," he said courteously to the other doctor, and bowing to him, he would have gone around him and away.

"*My* diagnosis," cried Dr. Alexander, "would be agranulocytosis!" He lifted his head, almost pranced, so pleased was he at having delivered that shaft.

Dr. Damery bowed again. "Excuse me, please," he said softly, and this time he managed to get around Dr. Alexander. His eyeglasses were flashing like headlights when he regained the open air. "Whew!" he said softly below his breath. Back at the hospital, he reminded Dr. Solley of his firm conviction that no doctor should ever attend a patient's funeral.

Peter asked his father-in-law to repeat, then spell, the long word which he had hurled at Dr. Damery.

Dr. Alexander repeated it, but said he'd not even try to spell it. "I think they want us to get into the limousine," he said importantly.

But once in the car, Peter asked him again what the word was, and what it meant.

Dr. Alexander glanced at his daughter, at Mark Sherwin's widow, and at Mrs. Alexander, all sitting in the big car's back seat. He and Peter occupied the jump seats.

He lifted his chin. "It's a big word for a doctor-induced illness!" he said emphatically.

His wife, who never understood these matters, gasped and laughed a little. Victoria gazed out of the window. Helen shook her head at her father. "You really shouldn't, Dad," she said softly.

"She's right," Peter agreed. "I—we—all of us gave my father the best care possible. If he had told the dentist about the medicine he was taking, or had told any of us about having that tooth pulled . . ."

91

"He didn't mention a toothache," said Victoria. "I'd asked him what was bothering him. I would never have gone to New York . . ."

"Of course you wouldn't," Helen comforted her. "But the doctors say he made another mistake in not staying at the hospital when he first collapsed. Tests then would have . . ."

"Alibis," Peter broke in. "These doctors—especially Gordie Damery—they jockey around, avoiding blame for the miserable service they gave my father!"

"Peter!" murmured his mother.

"I can't help it, Mom!" her son cried. "It was a run-around from the first! Why in the devil wasn't Gordie on the job when we needed him?"

"It was Sunday, dear. I don't blame him. He has always been our good friend."

"You may be able to look at things so. I'm afraid I can't. Couldn't Gordie have found a football game here in the city? Where he could have been reached for a case like this?"

"He's a surgeon . . ."

"Glamor boy," put in Dr. Alexander

"He's considered to be an especially fine surgeon, Dad," said Helen. "He must work under tremendous strain."

"I know all about the strain doctors work under, my dear. They should be ready to endure it. Damery claims Mark was not his patient—but what other doctors did care for the man?"

"Dad . . ." Peter began.

"I know he walked out," said Dr. Alexander. "But the

92

hospital should have stopped him; they could have cared for him."

"Against his will?" asked Peter. "You'd have the makings of a fine lawsuit there."

"I think his family has the makings of a fine lawsuit as things stand," said Dr. Alexander, nodding in satisfaction with himself.

Peter listened. He thought the matter over. His father should have been cared for, no matter what he said or did. In the extremities of his illness— He found out how to spell agranulocytosis, and wrote the word down in his memo book.

He was greatly grieved at his father's death; he seemed to resent the fact of that death as being unfair, unjustified. It could have been prevented, he decided. Other deaths like it should be prevented.

And before very long he was discussing this situation with everyone who would listen—with his friends, with his father's associates, and inevitably with representatives of the local newspapers.

This of course created a flurry. The Sherwins were prominent. Peter himself was an attorney. A judge. Did he plan a lawsuit? Against whom?

He did not commit himself or name anyone specifically. But it was known that Mark had died at St. Jerome's; it was easily determined that Dr. Damery had admitted him there. The death certificate was signed by a resident doctor in cardiovascular medicine. Dr. Perry was in Russia. Dr. Damery had gone to a Sunday football game.

Gordon Damery read the cleverly worded articles in the

93

newspapers, and he angrily called his friend to the telephone. What in hell, he asked, was Peter trying to do?

Peter was cool, then he was evasive. He finally said he was pretty sure his father would still be alive if he had had better care.

"And you consider yourself competent to judge?"

"I have medical opinions to bolster my belief."

Gordie was sure he knew where those medical opinions originated. "You know what I think, Peter?" the surgeon asked. "I think you'd do better to stick to the law. I am sure—I hope I am sure—that you know more about that."

He was angry.

When he repeated the telephone conversation to his wife, Peter told Helen that Gordie had been angry.

Helen Sherwin . . .

At the time, Mathilda Roberts thought—and she still thought, two years later—that Helen Sherwin, the daughter of a physician, an intelligent young woman who knew that publicity for a doctor and for a hospital was always bad, had, for that reason, tried to adjust matters between Dr. Damery and Peter.

Once, she was to remember, she had overheard Dr. Damery discussing the situation with Brook Solley. The two men were in scrub, their voices raised above the noise of the rushing water. Mathilda was busy in o.r., probably setting out bundles of instruments, linens, and utensils prior to surgery.

She had heard Dr. Damery say something about Helen Sherwin's inflated admiration of her father. "I'd be the last one to set her straight," he'd said, "but you would think she could read that man more truthfully."

94

Brook had said something about Oedipus, and Dr. Damery had ripped off some language that made Mathilda's eyebrows climb. He certainly was hot on the subject of the Sherwins. Dr. Solley had laughed about the vigor of his response.

Then she thought Dr. Damery had said something about being glad that Peter sometimes listened to his wife. "I think she may get the fella quieted down."

Mathilda hoped so. And when things did quiet down, she admired young Mrs. Sherwin for her skill.

They had quieted. Things.

After the first newspaper article or two, there had been no public discussion of Mark Sherwin's death. At the hospital, no files were set aside as secret or restricted. There seemed to be nothing except some talk in the hospital, especially in Thoracic, about Mr. Sherwin. His walk on the grounds was remembered and laughed about; the dietitian told about his ideas on food trays. An orderly remembered how he'd left the hospital that last Sunday. "Wouldn't have no part o' no wheelchair!" he'd tell. "He was a sick man, but he jest walked out!"

And within days, even this sort of talk subsided and gradually died.

That was the Sherwin story, so far as Mathilda knew it or had ever known it. First hand, she had no knowledge of it. The X-rated promenade through the hospital grounds, the matter of the abscessed tooth for a heart patient on heparin, had become hospital legend.

Could one write a book about such items? Could her having recounted such small incidents have inspired Dan

95

Kearnes to write a novel, to submit it for publication and have it accepted? She didn't know.

So she would ask Brook, who seemed in his quiet way to know a great deal about a great many things.

And on that summer morning she did ask him. They were dismissing a patient after open heart surgery. Dr. Solley liked to take these patients downstairs, outside, and to see them into a car, homeward-bound. "I wish it were Mrs. Bailey," he said, lingering for a last whiff of the warm summer sunshine, a last look at the brilliant blue sky. "All over and done with for her."

This morning, upstairs, he had asked Mathilda to "push the chair."

"He's the lazy type," she had told the smiling nurses at the station.

All concerned approved of the romance between Dr. Solley and the popular o.r. head.

Now they talked a little about Mrs. Bailey, and then about women doctors. The patient just dismissed had brought up the subject.

They guided the empty chair across the stretch of concrete; Brook held the door, and Mathilda pushed it through. Progress must be slow because of the number of people down on the first floor at that hour of the morning. Complete with families, new patients were coming in, florist delivery men, detail men, patients being discharged in their own wheelchairs, with their own families, nurses —sometimes a doctor.

"She said she was a doctor's daughter, but that her father had not encouraged her to study medicine," mused Mathilda. "But he did encourage his son."

96

"That was twenty years ago. I think he might take a different stand now," said Brook. "The percentages have improved."

"What changed the fathers' minds?"

"I don't think anything changed their minds. They probably are as stubborn and narrowminded as ever. What's changed is the girls."

"You've made a survey?" asked Mathilda saucily.

The lines around his mouth relaxed in what, for Brook, was a smile. "All the time," he assured her. "Look out, girl. You'll get a philodendron in your lap!"

Mathilda looked back at the laden delivery boy. "Was it a philodendron?"

"Certainly. All plants without flowers are philodendrons. There's more interest today, among young people, in service, and interest in science has grown among college students. Women students."

There was a mob at the elevators. Brook leaned against the far wall. "They're doing more in the study of fundamentals like math, physics, and physical chemistry. With that they can approach almost any field of science."

"Is that all it takes?"

"Of course not. But if they have that background, and add to it some native ability, and dedication, they can study medicine and not ask for Papa's approval."

"Just his pocketbook."

"I figure if I could make it on nothing, anybody can."

"It's harder for a girl."

"Yes, it is. Because, for one thing, she is apt to have heavier personal and social responsibilities."

"And the bank doesn't think she'll stick to it."

97

"Yes. That's why you made your silly promise not to get married until you'd cleared up the debt."

"I didn't think it was a silly promise."

"If you'd transfer that remaining debt to me, we could stop worrying about it."

"That would be nice. Do you think women make as good doctors as men?"

"No reason why they shouldn't. I wish we had five more up on Cardiac."

"Five," breathed Mathilda. *"Whhooee!"* She edged toward the elevator.

"You girls don't like 'em because you can't flirt with them and wheedle them."

"You are *smart,* Doctor!" said Miss Roberts. "Now that we've settled that point, can you find some smartness left over and tell me how Dan Kearnes could write a whole book . . . ?

"I think you're mistaken," she concluded. "The Sherwin case just couldn't make a book. Just that episode."

"Yes, it would," said Dr. Solley, taking charge of the wheelchair and steering it into the elevator. "Will you please take the next car?" he asked the three people who still wanted to ride up.

He pushed buttons. These elevators thought for themselves. And though he had indicated the twelfth floor, eventually, first they went to the basement; he kept the door closed. They went to the sixteenth floor, down to the fifth . . .

And he talked fast. "It would make a book, Tillie," he said. "It has made one. That episode, that story, Mr. Sherwin's death, and what happened afterward."

Her eyes were wide and round. She stared at Brook. "What do you mean?"

"That there has been no forgiving or forgetting in the Sherwin household. Not by the son, the widow, the son's wife, or his father-in-law."

Mentally, Mathilda placed and named these characters. "Do you think now they will revive—that they will file a suit?"

"Not against Damery," said Brook, still busy with buttons.

"Then— Oh, you mean against Dan."

"If he publishes the book. Fichter is sure, and I am sure, that Peter Sherwin will sue the hospital."

There must have been a conference.

"Then," Mathilda agreed, "he would have to withdraw it."

But she was already grieving. Thinking of Dan, by now probably finished with his interview with the Administrator, knowing how crushed the ebullient young man would be—must be.

Chapter Five

ONE approached the Hospital Administrator's office —Dan Kearnes reached it that beautiful summer morning—through an open array of desks and typewriters, between the partially enclosed cubicles of various officers—the Personnel Director, the Treasurer, the Purchasing Officer, and so on. Finally one came into the large, hushed area of the Administrator's offices. There a receptionist sat at the entrance to the waiting room, an attractive young woman, friendly to a point, who smiled at Dan and asked him please to wait. "It won't be long," she assured him, lifting the phone.

Dan had dressed carefully for this interview, and he hoped he seemed to be more self-assured than he was. If only he knew what was *up!* He found a chair, one of several comfortable leather ones. There was a long leather couch against the opposite wall; the carpet was a muted red; there were pictures on the walls, shaded lamps on small tables, available reading matter, and two other men, also waiting.

Dan held a magazine and tried not to fidget. If he knew what the meeting would be about, he could plan what he would say. Would anyone but himself and Fichter be present? He knew Fichter, having had discussions with him on various subjects. New techniques in cataract surgery, a new treatment center for retarded children, the use of laser in surgery . . .

But never before had he discussed the book which the young reporter himself had had the temerity to write.

And why shouldn't he have written it? Books were being written all the time! Quite controversial ones, too. Books with characters that were easily, even nationally, identifiable. Why should St. Jerome's Hospital be immune? Dan visited various hospitals. If you described one, you pictured them all! The waiting room of this administrator had a red carpet. So what?

The thing would be not to let Fichter intimidate him. Dan had his rights. He had already resigned from the paper, so what threat or danger could there be? He must keep these things in his mind.

"Mr. Kearnes," said the receptionist's clear voice, "you may go in now." Her pencil pointed to the door beside the long table which held magazines, a red and blue Chinese-type jar, and a low bowl of flowers—chrysanthemums or zinnias, or some such.

He jumped to his feet, pulled down his jacket, said "Sorry" to the two men who still must wait, said "Thank you, love" to the receptionist, who smiled. And he walked briskly across to the door, opened it, let it suck closed behind him. He went down the narrow, short corridor to where Mr. Fichter's secretary sat.

"Good morning, Mrs. Wafford," he said briskly. "How are you this bright and beautiful morning?"

Mrs. Wafford, a divorcee, was probably forty, though women, these days . . . She was slender, her gray-streaked blonde hair was neither disheveled nor rigidly coiffed. Her

101

makeup was subdued.

She nodded to Dan and pointed *her* pencil to the door of Mr. Fichter.

"My slip isn't showing, is it?" Dan asked her.

"Mr. Fichter is waiting."

"Oh, then . . ." He did a little change step and opened the door—THE DOOR.

Behind him, Mrs. Wafford sighed just a little. She rather liked Dan Kearnes, brash and irrepressible though he was.

Dan felt of his brown and gold striped tie as he opened the door into Mr. Fichter's office. He knew that he was being silly and he knew that he was silly because he was nervous. Perhaps the one thing would counteract the other. But he didn't think so.

Mr. Fichter sat behind his large desk, and he glanced up as Dan entered. "Sit down, will you, Kearnes?" he asked.

Dan sat down in the chair placed at the corner of the desk. He looked around the office. Behind Fichter was a wall of what he had learned was linen-fold paneling; at each corner of the room, breaking into this wall, were doors. One led to a short hall which in turn led to the main corridor of the building. Thus, departing visitors did not need to go through the waiting room "Heads up, or tails down," thought Dan.

The second door, he supposed, led to Fichter's personal coat rack and toilet—maybe even a shower. They did things well at St. Jerome's. Perhaps there was a refrigerator and drinks . . .

Mr. Fichter looked busy. But the man also was nervous. Dan could tell. He kept stealing glances at Dan, and he

102

dropped his pencil twice, fumbled when he picked it up. He signed some papers, stacked one on top of the other arranged so that he need see only the space above the typed name. He lifted the telephone and asked to be connected with a person named Voshak. Was there anyone with such a name?

Yes, there was. Because Fichter was speaking sharply to someone about the proper presentation of bills, which should be accompanied by a carbon of the requisition . . . some rigamarole of hospital business.

Dan stared at Mr. Fichter. The man was round, he decided—round head; round, compact body; round, pudgy fists. He was bald and richly tanned. He was not a handsome man, but pleasant-looking. Restrained, controlled. He dressed well. Today's suit was gray-blue, his shirt was gray, and his tie plain blue. Yes, restrained.

Next, Fichter took an incoming telephone call. This was what Dan identified as a family interruption. Fichter's wife had had a letter from their daughter—named Peggy —who was making excuses for not coming home this summer. No, Mr. Fichter was not interested in joining Peggy and Jack for a weekend. "Tell her I think she owes us a few days here," he said firmly. "We should see our grandchild more than once a year."

Hmmmn. So this stuffed shirt had a wife, a daughter, and even a grandchild.

And he certainly was all bottled up. What means did the guy have of relieving pressure? Dan should look into Fichter's background—where he lived, how he played—if he played. What was his wife like? He didn't blame "Peggy" for not wanting to spend much time with—

103

Fichter was clearing his throat, and Dan sprang to attention.

"Yes, sir!" he said. He almost saluted, but was thankful that he had not. Fichter was in no mood to be amused.

The Administrator was leaning back in his chair, gazing at the reporter.

"This book you have written," he said quietly, "is it about the hospital?"

"Oh, no, sir," said Dan quickly. "Its setting is *a* hospital, but I was thinking, when I came in this morning, that all hospitals are pretty much alike. Wouldn't you agree?"

"No," said Mr. Fichter.

Dan gulped.

"When did you write this novel, Kearnes?"

"Oh, in the evenings, on weekends, vacations. I worked on it for a couple of years."

"I see. Could you give me some idea of its plot?"

"I could, I suppose. I'm not good at outlines. I mean, I work out the whole thing while trying to tell what the idea is."

"Would you have a copy I could read?"

"Well, yes, sir, but—Yeah. I have a copy at home."

"Mhmmmn. I indicated last night that the publisher had called me. He had learned that you covered several hospitals in your daily reporting work."

"I told him that I did. They asked for a short autobiography. And references, as well."

"I see. Your publisher seems to be better at sketching outlines; he had no difficulty indicating the basis for your story."

Dan wondered what he had said. "It's about the intrusion of personal matters on the busy life of professional people, sir."

"Yes." Fichter's fingertips tapped the telephone. "And like that call I just had from my wife, they do intrude."

"Oh, but—"

"I know. You didn't write a book about a small domestic problem."

The Administrator leaned back in his chair and regarded the young reporter. "I understand it gives a person a wonderful feeling to write a book and have it accepted for publication."

Dan's head lifted, and a smile brightened his face. "Yes, sir!" he agreed. "It is great."

"Mhmmmn. Now, it would seem, you have done your work, and the publisher must take over. To edit, to print, to sell the book. Is that the way things go?"

"Well, I suppose so, sir. I'm new at the business."

"I recognize that. And the publisher does—evidently. I think he was admirably astute to check with the hospitals with which you've become familiar in your reporting."

"He could have checked with me, saved himself quite a heap of telephone bills."

Mr. Fichter smiled faintly. "Would you have told him the source of your story?"

Dan shrugged. "I suppose so. Why not? I felt, I do feel, that I had a right to use the story. It was only an idea, really, a minor part of the whole story told. I built that story myself. This idea came to my attention, and I developed it—all fiction, sir. Every bit of it. There are no recognizable pictures drawn."

"When the publisher talked to me, I had no difficulty

105

identifying the malpractice case." Fichter's voice was cold.

Dan sat up straight in his chair. "Who mentioned malpractice?" he asked.

The Administrator was human, after all. He could be flustered, and he was. He coughed to cover this revelation. He colored—not much, but enough. He reached for a pencil and became interested in writing something on his memo pad. Evidently he had said more than he had planned to say. Now the ball was his, and he had to do something with it.

He lifted his head, reaching for the fishy expression which he found so useful when dealing with situations such as he had this morning. Well, he never had had exactly this situation before. He coughed again.

"I told you," he reminded young Kearnes, "that your publisher had called me and briefly outlined the story you were telling in your book. Enough of it that I was immediately aware that a malpractice case, if not *in* the book, could be developed *from* it. As you must know, all hospitals are liable to that attack, and from all sides. It is a constant hazard and one against which we continually must be on guard. I'm not at all happy to think that such a case could develop from the first literary effort of a reporter to whom this hospital has extended a few courtesies, carefully restricted and defined."

He's mad as hell, Dan told himself. Scared, and mad. Mad because he was scared, probably. Dan himself wondered what he had got himself into, and whether he'd be able to get himself out.

"I'm afraid you've lost me, sir," he managed to say, his

voice not especially firm.

Mr. Fichter glanced at him. "Did you expect me to *like* what you seem to have done to me, Kearnes?" he asked.

"I don't know, sir. I still am in the dark . . ."

"Well, I wish I were there with you," cried the angry man. "I'd like to hide from the suspicion—and I can promise that just the suspicion makes me damn mad, Kearnes—to think that any happening in my hospital—*any happening at all*—could be revealed to a newspaper reporter like yourself!"

His tone was not complimentary, and it was Dan's turn to flush. "I'm a very good reporter, sir," he said stiffly. "I've worked up to being one. I can spot an item of interest for myself, and develop it. In the past, you've complemented me for the way I've found out things for myself in rounding out a story. You will remember the series I did about the volunteers here at the hospital."

"Yes, yes!" cried Fichter. "But this matter is entirely different. Someone here in the hospital told you what you call the idea for your book, gave you the seed from which your novel grew. And—well—quite frankly, I am asking you if you will identify that person, that informant."

Dan stared at the man across the desktop. This interview was taking a very ugly turn. He was startled at the suggestion that his book might make trouble for anyone, shocked at the suggestion that he would reveal unspeakable things, and frightened at the promise of reprisal for anyone, against himself, or anyone even more innocent of doing an unwise thing.

"Of course I won't identify anyone!" he shouted. "I'm not saying I did get the idea for my novel from anyone

107

here at St. Jerome's. I certainly haven't said that I did! As a matter of truth, sir, I have had that 'seed,' as you aptly called it, in my consciousness for some time! It was just an incident—one hears these little stories—it takes months and months, you know, to write a book. It took me almost two years, because I did it in my spare time. It isn't only the writing, the typing, and all. But the development of the plot. The seed of the story has to be planted and allowed to grow in the writer's mind." Now he had forgotten his fear and his shock. That *was* the way his book had grown. "There was this incident, yes, sir, there was. But the book's plot, the story told, is all fiction. Purely imagination!"

"The publisher and I agreed that your story began with a situation so close to the truth that it could be identified, and people involved could sue the hospital for telling—"

"What *happened*, Mr. Fichter, was something I made up! It is fiction!"

"How close to the truth did it come? The story you developed?"

"I don't know, sir. If it comes close at all, it is a coincidence, or based on the logical laws of human behavior."

"Will the readers who identify the actual person and the 'small happening' know that the 'story' you developed is imaginary?"

"Why, sure. At least, they should."

"There was a family involved, Kearnes. They'll know, as I do, that people are very nimble at jumping to conclusions."

Kearnes opened his mouth to protest, then sat back in his chair, stricken.

108

"I am grateful," said Mr. Fichter, "that your publisher is so careful, that he checked names and called the hospitals for fear of—I am quoting his exact words, Kearnes—'for fear of a possible suit around the story of a man, a former heart patient, who checked back into the hospital hemorrhaging because of a recently extracted tooth; he had not told the dentist he was on anticoagulants. In his delirium, he escaped from the hospital, and certain things happened to him and to his family.' "

"Imaginary things," said Dan glumly, stubbornly. "The story of the book itself is pure fiction."

"But—you see, Kearnes, I recognize the incident of the heart patient hemorrhaging from the extracted tooth, getting out into the grounds—the family and friends of the man will recognize it—and I want to know, I am asking you to tell me—where you heard *that* part of your story."

"And I am refusing to tell you," said Dan, more stubbornly than before.

"Did you know the man, the patient, involved?"

"No! I hardly ever know any patient!"

"Just the staff and the personnel of the hospital," said Fichter coldly.

"It was a small item, sir. I expect a dozen or more people talked about it."

"And one of that dozen talked to you."

"Well, let's say I heard it."

The Administrator was very angry. He got out of his big leather chair and paced around the office. He told Dan that he would never again be allowed to set foot in St. Jerome's. He said he would probably institute a lawsuit himself. And he promised . . .

109

"I will find out who is to blame, Kearnes," he said roughly. "In fact, I feel that I already know who is to blame. I know, I have determined, who your friends are here in the hospital. I know the people to whom you talk, with whom you consort . . ."

Consort. Now that was one hell of a word! What did the fellow have in mind? An affair? A dinner date?

Dan felt his limbs stiffen and go cold.

". . . can promise you that the person will suffer!" cried the Administrator.

Dan stared at him, more shocked than he had thought he could be. If this hard-nosed man ever got it into his round head— Dan knew how ruthlessly Fichter had sought and secured the position as Administrator. If he . . . ever . . .

The telephone buzzed, and Mr. Fichter answered it, sitting down again in his chair to talk to the caller. He talked for ten minutes about the benefit golf tournament always given in August to support the charitable services of the children's unit of St. Jerome's.

Dan listened, not really hearing, and he watched Mr. Fichter. He tried to think of synonyms for *ruthless.* There just wasn't any other word as good for Fichter. If he knew who had told Dan—if he could find out—Fichter was capable of some rough punishment against the person who would hazard the good name, the shining reputation, of St. Jerome's.

". . . I know the people to whom you talk, with whom you consort."

That dinner date with Mathilda! Had Dan talked about that? He could have. Mathilda herself had told Solley.

110

Solley, angry, even jealous, might have said a thing or two to his friends in protest. Mathilda might have bragged a little, a very little. Just—"Dan Kearnes has written a book and he's asked me to have dinner with him to celebrate." Yes, she could have said that.

And a ruthless man like Fichter—Mathilda up on Cardiovascular would have known about the "incident" of the guy who didn't tell about his tooth, and who took a stroll through the grounds . . .

The most dangerous thing was: Mathilda had told Dan about that happening. Dan had made a note of it. He was storing up hospital incidents to put into his fiction writing. When inviting Mathilda to dinner, he'd explained that she had "helped him write the book." Someone could have overheard him say that, or Tillie could have told someone. She *had* told Solley. And Solley, jealous of Dan, would be ready to tell Fichter, not realizing that he would hurt his girl so dreadfully.

Because Fichter would hurt her! And that was not fair. Mathilda was a great girl. Dan had liked her ever since his first sight of her. Even in the horrible o.r. getup she looked cute. She always had a cheery word for a guy; she was truly concerned for her patients. And last night she had been as worried as Dan was about the call from the Administrator. She probably was worrying right now, wondering about the interview.

He certainly did not want to hurt Mathilda. If ever Dan would decide to pick one girl, to marry her, it would be a girl like Mathilda Roberts. Cute, sweet, capable. Honest. It would be Mathilda, if that were at all possible. And he was as certain as he could be that he didn't want—he never had wanted—to hurt that girl!

She had so enjoyed her dinner the night before. Her little red slippers had twinkled when they danced, and she had fairly gobbled the antipasto. No, sir, he was not going to let Mathilda be hurt.

Mr. Fichter finished with the telephone call and made a few notes on his memo pad. When he glanced at Dan, the young man was ready for him.

"I wish you would tell me," Dan said briskly, "who you think gave me that little incidental story about a patient."

Fichter's eyes bulged. "I can't tell you any such thing!" he cried indignantly.

"But you have to, sir. I wouldn't do more than affirm or deny the truth."

Dan's skill as a reporter now came to his aid. After a bit of skirmishing . . .

"I can't tell you!"

"You *must* tell me!"

. . . Richter conceded that a nurse was overheard talking to a resident about Dan's book, about the source of the story he'd used—in the cafeteria, this was. And, in fact, both nurse and resident seemed to be guilty of talking too much, and . . .

"And your spies told you."

Fichter had the grace to flush, but his voice stayed hard. "It is my job," he said coldly, "to keep my hand on the threads."

Yes, he was near enough to the truth. Too near, in fact. There was no escape, no shading the possibility. Dan felt panic rising about him like fog. What was happening to him? What terrible thing had he done? What unbelievable

112

thing would he do if his book were published? Why, any lawsuit about its subject matter would surely involve his friends, and would destroy them. Mathilda, Dr. Solley—the publishers themselves—would know only disaster and destruction. He could see no way out! The medical profession was too vulnerable; it could not be a matter of assault, of accusation.

Dan stood up, feeling his strong limbs weak, the palms of his hands wet. "I think I have only one course to take, Mr. Fichter," he said, his voice hoarse in his throat. "And that would be to withdraw my book from publication."

His capitulation had caught Fichter unready for such a step. "Not publish the book at all?" he asked in disbelief. All he had hoped for was a change, a rewriting.

"Would your publisher allow that?" he asked. "I understand there was a contract . . ."

"Yes, and an advance paid. But—of course I don't know if the publisher will agree. I would have to ask him —them."

"And you would do that?" Even in his agitation, his excitement, Dan could detect the relief in Fichter's voice and in his eyes. Why, the man had been scared. Maybe . . .

No! He was doing the only possible thing. "Yes," he agreed. "I will call the publisher and tell him that this issue has been raised . . ."

"He knows it had better be," agreed Mr. Fichter. "Suppose we call the publisher now, from this phone."

"Well . . ." said Dan.

"It would clear the whole thing up once and for all. Then you could get to work, rewriting your book, or

113

starting on a new one."

Dan did not want Fichter telling him what to do! He should be informed that this sacrifice was not being made for him, nor for Jerome's. It was for Mathilda, and for her alone. And he could not say that.

Numb with his pain, his disappointment, he watched and listened to the Administrator ask to have the call made to New York.

"Would you like some coffee?" Fichter asked him. "We may have a wait . . ."

Dan, by then, was standing against the draperies at the long window. "No!" he said gruffly. "Nothing."

He turned and stared out of the window. The glass curtains were sheer, flecked with threads of color—but one could see the front main entrance to St. Jerome's. A fountain bubbled, cars pulled up—a nurse in white shoes crossed the driveway.

And the call came through. Fichter talked first, then handed the phone to Dan, who had not the vaguest thought about what to say.

But he must have said it. Because the publisher's voice —still friendly—was saying something too about a rewrite job. "Oh, no one's to blame, Kearnes. First book authors all have to learn certain facts of life."

Dan offered to return the check. The publisher said perhaps he should keep it against his next book. "You write well. We'd like to have you on our list."

"I'll return the check," said Dan, and he handed the phone back to Fichter.

Even as he did so, he saw the blinking red light among the buttons on Fichter's desk. Fichter saw it too, and snatched the phone. "I'm sorry," he said to Dan. "I will have to talk to you again later." He pressed buttons, he talked, he listened. Dan watched him. There definitely was an emergency.

This was confirmed as he made his way out of the Administrator's office. Out in the hall where agitation was mounting in waves, he caught the word *blackout.*

At eleven o'clock? On a sunny day?

". . . power failure . . ."

But lights were on, the elevators seemed to be working here in the main lobby.

Still—Fichter passed him like a hot wind. Now people were coming from all directions. There was a siren, sounding not like an ambulance . . .

A reporter by talent and training, Dan knew how to move and ask questions, too. Yes, there had been a power failure—a blackout, really—in Emergency Receiving, and in Cardiac . . .

He ran. All morning his thoughts had been on Mathilda. If Cardiac . . . Emergency was in the building adjacent to Cardiac . . .

More and more people were milling about—personnel, visitors, delivery men. Real panic threatened. A general disaster alarm was sounding, and a firetruck screamed up as Dan raced from the main building's driveway to the cardiac building. Someone pointed upward. Smoke and some flames were coming from the elevator shaft. There would be intensive care patients—and Mathilda.

Dan had just one thought, to reach Mathilda—to rescue her, he later supposed. At the actual minute, he had no plan, other than to evade the guards, the nurses, the or-

115

derlies—and to get upstairs.

No elevators were running in Cardiac-Vascular, and the corridors were indeed "blacked out" in broad daylight. Some measure of discipline was being restored. Visitors were being herded to the sunrooms. "Watch for cigarettes," said someone. Yes. Oxygen would be a problem. Nurses and orderlies took their positions.

The whole thing was like a nightmare—to Dan, and to everyone else. One ran, and got nowhere. People spoke, screamed even, and no sound came through to change anything. There was panic and order all at the same time.

The blackout, which was to last for two hours, was a fluky thing. Later it was attributed to a break in one of two cables supplying power from a substation. The diesel-powered auxiliary power unit of the hospital engaged immediately. However, it did not transfer power to two of the buildings because the power failure was not complete. Mr. Fichter himself made that explanation. The city, the county, Dan Kearnes, Brook Solley and Mathilda Roberts were to read about all that later. That particular noontime each of the three individuals was too busy. "We were extremely fortunate that there was no surgery being performed at the time of the failure," said Mr. Fichter, properly identified in the newspaper article, which should have been phoned in by Dan Kearnes. He was on the scene; this would have been a scoop.

Instead, he was hunting Mathilda Roberts, for his own reasons.

"No births or deaths occurred in the two units involved."

Cardiac was involved, and with that unit, the chief

surgical resident and his o.r. nurse. The "thing" caught them involved in an intense fight to save the life of a patient who had suffered cardiac arrest.

There were, in fact, no serious breakdowns in emergency or patient service. Many lighting devices, including cigarette lighters, were pressed into use.

At 11:13, just before the blackout began, a young man, Timothy Williams, an automobile accident victim, suffered cardiac arrest in the intensive care ward on the surgical floor of Cardiac where he had been taken from Emergency. Dr. Solley was summoned, even as the blackout occurred.

Under disaster conditions, Miss Roberts took her position in o.r. A tracheotomy was performed on young Williams, the resident and the nurses using lighting provided by two power generators, available for just such occasions.

"The work was extremely difficult," said Dr. Solley afterward. "We were just lucky."

Through with Williams, he grabbed Mathilda's hand, and they raced downstairs and across to Emergency. There could be other heart cases—"incidents"—and no elevators to transfer them up to Cardiac surgery.

In Emergency, together, they used eight stitches to sew up a cut, a nosebleed was stanched, and to their own amazement they took care of two rabies preventive services, and gave relief to an asthmatic.

"Our main problem here," said Brook, as he worked on that patient, "is oxygen. Unlike the units in the rooms and all over the hospital, an asthmatic inhaler requires power."

During the break, all arriving emergency cases were

117

diverted to other hospitals in the city. And after two hours service was restored. The break in the cable, said the power company crew, had occurred within the hospital itself.

"Just a disaster drill," said Brook Solley with relief. "A guy never appreciates little conveniences like elevators and a hot plate for his coffeepot until the juice goes off."

After two hours, reporters had to be combed out of the place, but Dan Kearnes was still feeling that he should have made the scoop. He'd been there at the first alarm! He had actually directed firemen through the corridors and the stairways. He—

But he was no longer a reporter, he no longer was a feature writer. All he wanted to do was to see that Mathilda was safe. Then—he would tell her—

The lights were going on, flaring up beautifully white, flickering—with everyone looking anxiously at the ceiling and breathing lightly. The tubes faded out, then shone bright again, and stayed that way. A faint cheer went up. "Let's everybody go to lunch!" said one of the staff doctors who had been valiantly helping, going from bed to bed reassuring the patients.

"Naw, there's no fire!" he said to each one. "Everything will be fine in a few minutes."

It had helped. Everything helped.

Now he was calling his office and his home. "In case you heard and wondered what I'd done to make things break down," he told his wife. "Why, sure I'm fine. Sure I was in the hospital. They needed someone to be here, didn't they?"

Everyone was smiling at him.

118

The doctor put the phone down and glanced at Dan. "Can I do something for you, Kearnes?" he asked.

"Thank you, Dr. Light," said Dan. "I was going to ask if I could see Miss Roberts."

"Oh, I wouldn't know that!" said Dr. Light. "She's been helping down in Emergency. Maybe she went off with a policeman." He started away down the hall.

Dan turned to ask the charge nurse; Brook Solley, who had come up to the chart desk, heard him. When he went on to o.r.—Mathilda would be there, checking every autoclave and dial in the place!—he told her that Dan was out at the desk asking to see her.

Mathilda looked up. "What does he want?"

"How should I know? Probably another date."

Mathilda made a face at him. "You have a one-track mind," she said. Dan certainly wanted to tell her about his interview with Fichter. Maybe the Administrator had blown all the fuses.

"I'll check these valves with you," Brook offered.

"They seem to be in order. I think I'll reset all the autoclaves, just to be sure."

"Make the dressings room, too," said Brook. "And Central Supply."

He did not want her to see Dan. But of course she had to, if only to quiet down her curiosity.

And with everything ticking or hissing or just sitting there ready, she pulled off her cap and went out to see Dan.

Chapter Six

MATHILDA looked along the hall. Brook was nowhere in sight. She didn't think he had gone for lunch.

She went to the desk, asked to see the schedule, which she had already seen in scrub. She was free until two-thirty; she should get some lunch.

"Dr. Solley?" she asked the charge nurse.

"D'you lose him, Roberts?"

Mathilda smiled at the woman. "That's hard to do," she said sweetly.

"Oh, he's in his office."

"Good." By then she had located Dan, leaning against the wall, down by the elevators. "I'm going down for lunch," she told the nurse. "And I most certainly will be back by two-fifteen."

She walked quickly to the elevators, nodded to Dan, who followed her in.

"Lunch," she said, "and talk fast. Team comes on at two-thirty."

"You're going to work late?"

"Why should today be different? What happened . . . ?" She broke off because three people got on at 10.

They went to the cafeteria, which was packed, but

120

Mathilda found two places. She had selected a sandwich, apple salad and a slice of cake. Dan brought two glasses of iced tea.

"No appetite?" Mathilda asked him sadly.

"That's right." He had not smiled once. His clothes looked a little rumpled.

"Did you help during the two hours?" she asked briskly, cutting her sandwich.

"A little. I was waiting to see you. Look, could we wait to talk until you've finished tonight?"

"I'll be bushed. And I don't think going to your apartment agrees with me. I didn't sleep a wink last night."

"I'm sorry. I—" He drank some tea. Mathilda glanced up at him.

"Tell me what happened," she said quietly. "With Fichter."

He looked around. "This place is full of spies," he told Mathilda, his tone as solemn as his face.

"Didn't you know that?"

"Not really," he said. "But let me tell you . . ."

So he did tell her, Mathilda watching his face and trying to eat her lunch. Their bypass could take hours, and she couldn't remember eating breakfast.

She listened, and she watched Dan, and by the minute her face became more concerned. She made few comments, even to agree with Dan when he said Fichter was a Gestapo. "I never saw such a cold person!" he declared. "He just doesn't give a damn about other warm-blooded people. He can't bleed, so he thinks no one else can."

"He knows they can," murmured Mathilda.

"Well, maybe. But he doesn't *care!* Mathilda, that man was ready to involve you and Solley, and punish you both!"

The tiny golden freckles popped out green on her face. "Brook hadn't a thing to do with it!" she cried.

"Did he talk to you about it? Recently?"

She stared at him. "Ye-es," she agreed. "He told me I should not talk about things that happened here in the hospital. That was yesterday. We had a break. We talked about the date with me to tell me about your book."

Dan groaned. His *book!* "Boy," he cried, "I wish I had never learned to write!"

"Oh, Dan . . . What did he do to you?"

"He couldn't *do* very much to me. I'd already quit my job here. But he wanted to get at you, Tillie, and at Dr. Solley. To punish you for talking to me."

"Brook didn't."

"I know he didn't. But Fichter—I just couldn't let that happen, you know. I'd told him that I'd only picked up the one small item and invented all the rest of the story. He would not listen to me! He was scared about my book. To prevent a lawsuit, the publishers had checked, and this threw him into a panic. He talked to various people, and one of them had overheard you and Solley . . ."

"Yes. You told me I'd given you the item. Maybe someone heard *you*—"

"They could have. Certainly I had no intent of hurting you. And I told him so. And then I offered not to publish the book."

"Oh, Dan . . ." She sounded so very sorry. She glanced up at him. "Now *you* are being punished."

"Yes, and I don't think I should be. One should be able to pick up details, turn them around, and write about them."

"I'm sure you could. I don't see why they should punish you."

"Well, I suppose because I wrote the damn book. You didn't."

"But if Fichter thinks Brook and I talk too much . . ."

"I told him you didn't. I told him I'd heard the little story from a half-dozen people."

"And I'll bet you did, too."

"Yes, I did. For all the good it did me."

Mathilda swiftly touched the back of his hand. "I *am* sorry, Dan!"

"Yeah. So am I. You see, Mathilda—while the loss of money is a big item with me, the loss of the prestige is even bigger. I felt I had finally found a way to do something that would set me out a little, that would make people notice me and speak of me. And not just *people*, either. I thought I was gaining an edge with a lot of special people."

"Me?" she asked ingenuously.

He managed a smile for her. "Well, yes, *you*. Of course. I liked your being proud of me, of saying you were proud. That was swell. But there was still another thing. The book was going to be a—an—an ego builder for me."

She stared at him. Her eyes went swiftly to the clock and back to his face. Fifteen minutes. "Tell me what you mean," she urged.

"Well—we don't have much time. But— Have I ever talked to you about my family?"

123

"A little. Your mother is ten feet tall. And you have brothers."

"That about says it," he agreed. "My mother is all of ten feet tall, and beautiful. She is a very successful business woman. My two brothers are eggheads, but these days eggheads get places. One is written up as a boy-wonder financial wizard, and the other not only belongs to a think-tank research center, he *is* a think-tank! In electronics. Anyway, they are all wonderful. Good-looking, dynamic —everything that I am not. When I was in prep school, and then in college, I used to dream about being a famous criminal lawyer, and that my snobbish family—one of them, at least—would get into a serious jam, and they'd have to come to me for help."

Mathilda smiled at him. "You didn't even study law," she said.

"No, I didn't. And they wouldn't ever have got into a jam. But I did think my book would make a tiny, faint mark on this family of high achievers. And now—it isn't going to go, and I'll never be able to convince my snobbish family that they really are snobs—that a guy who ended his education without a Ph.D. could do *something!* Because now . . ."

"Did you really tell the publisher you wanted to withdraw the book?"

"I was frightened for you and Solley. Mainly you. I didn't want to be the cause of a scandal about the hospital, or the reason for you to lose your job."

"Oh, I wish— Why should you get so excited and do such a desperate thing? I don't believe the general public would connect your story with this hospital. Tell me again what happened this morning, Dan. Briefly, of course."

"Yes. Well, the publisher asked about the names I'd used for my characters. This alerted Fichter, who asked him what the story was about. He was told it dealt with a hushed-up malpractice suit, growing out of that abscessed tooth situation. I don't suppose he gave many details, but enough that Fichter recognized the thing."

Mathilda nodded. "And of course the Sherwin family might make the connection if they—one of them—happened to read the book."

"Oh, they would! The publisher would make a promotion thing of my being a reporter on this beat. The town would get curious, buy the book—they'd hope—and—"

Mathilda was watching the clock. "I don't think you should withdraw it," she said flatly.

"I was tempted not to. I was tempted, after I left Fichter's office, to call back and say I wouldn't. I maybe could have stood up to Fichter. I could maybe stand up to the publisher, if I had a little more experience. But this is—was—my first book, Mathilda. And I decided I couldn't do this thing and face all it would mean. That would take a very brave man. And I'm a coward."

Mathilda shook her head. "I do wish it had not worked out this way."

Dan reached for a paper napkin and patted his cheeks. "God!" he said reverently. "How I wish it hadn't!"

"I'd go on and publish it. And if there should be a lawsuit— Why, one would sell a million copies of your book!"

"And Fichter would fire you and blackball you."

125

"Oh, he was bluffing."

"I did use you, love."

She felt like weeping. "But not Brook. He was not in this at all. And my part—it was very small, Dan."

"It was enough."

She stood up, ready to leave. "I still think you could fight this thing. Brazen it out."

He shook his head. "The point is, I didn't."

"Because of me." She spoke sadly. Maybe she should be flattered. She knew girls who would be. "I think I could have weathered it," she said over her shoulder.

"I don't know, Tillie. Fichter said some chilling things. He used a phrase, 'Willfully releasing patient information.' "

"Oh, dear," said Mathilda, sucking in her breath.

"You've heard it before?"

"Yes. It is in the rules—professional behavior—all that jazz. We agree to comply with those rules."

"Solley, too?"

"I don't really know, but I suppose so. As a resident house staff . . ."

"That's right. And if there was a chance that you could be involved, you would have involved him."

"Why, I would not!"

"With a nudge from Fichter, I mean."

Mathilda shook her head and went out through the cafeteria doors into the hall. "You didn't mention your father," she said when Dan caught up with her. "You must have had one."

"I did," Dan agreed. "He—died. When I was eighteen. He wasn't a Ph.D. either."

126

Mathilda looked at him curiously. "Are your brothers as nice as you are?" she asked.

"Oh, Lord, Mathilda!"

"I was just wondering if they would do what you have done. I still marvel that the Administrator would, or could, exert so much pressure on you."

"He couldn't," said Dan. "He didn't. I was the one who thought about what a row over my book would mean, not only to you, but to Brook Solley, a resident on the service of the surgeon involved."

About to step into the elevator, Mathilda turned and came back to Dan; she drew him away from the group of people waiting to go up—or down.

She stared into Dan's face. "What on earth are you talking about?" she said in a fierce whisper. She urged him over to the edge of the corridor against the windows. "What surgeon?" she hissed. "Not . . ."

"Well, of course," said Dan. "You don't suppose I wrote a whole book about a man with a bad tooth, do you? My real reason was the romance, the mystery, the—"

"I don't know what you are talking about!" said Mathilda indignantly, running her fingers through her hair. It sprang up in little red-brown tendrils around them. "I'm going to be late, but you have to tell me. Romance? Mystery?"

"Yes. That was my incentive. The abscessed tooth and the malpractice suit which the Sher—, which that family threatened—that was only the takeoff, Tillie. The rest of the story was the important thing."

Mathilda gazed at him. She shook her head slowly from side to side. "I don't understand," she said faintly. "What

127

rest of what story?"

"Oh, you know. When that—er—tooth thing developed, there was a surgeon involved. I won't mention names. The family wanted him to take the case, but he was out of town, supposedly in Chicago at a football game."

Mathilda remembered. "Where *was* he?" she asked, dreading his answer, but demanding it anyway. Dr. Damery was like a god to her.

"You asked about the rest of the story—my story. I learned that the surgeon was not at a football game, and from that I developed a story and wrote the book—the why's, the what's, and the when's."

Mathilda pressed her shoulders against the window frame. No wonder Fichter wanted—demanded—that the book not be published. The surgeon involved was his first star, a world-famous man. St. Jerome's glowed in the bright light of his fame.

"There's never been a word of scandal about . . ." she began fiercely.

Swiftly Dan put his hand across her mouth. "Don't say it!" he said fiercely.

"You—you found out—" she sputtered.

"Sure I did. Remember, I was a reporter. And it didn't take too much to find out that he'd not gone to any football game, though he had gone to Chicago. And that's where the old imagination went to work. I developed the rest of my story logically, and possibly truthfully. Anyway, I set up and made a thing of the triangle involving him."

Mathilda's mouth fell open. "Damery?" she said silently.

128

"The surgeon," Dan corrected, reproving her.

"Who else? You said triangle."

"Yes. Well, there was a young woman involved in the original item, wasn't there? The daughter-in-law of the man who died; the husband would make the third leg. He threatened a suit for—for you-know-what. Of course, there's your triangle."

The husband, the daughter-in-law, and—

Mathilda stood stunned, though her mind conjured pictures.

She would not look at the corridor clock nor at her steel-cased wrist watch. Any minute now, the enunciator would begin to yell for her. She was really shattering every rule! She would be bounced off the team. Brook would not even speak to her after this.

She could hear his stern voice. "If you cannot be depended upon, Miss Roberts, you are of no value whatever to us."

"You said you made up the story . . ." she stuttered to Dan. "Then, if *that* part is not true . . ."

"I suspect it comes entirely too close to the truth. I did my best to find out what the surgeon was up to—going to Chicago—giving a false reason for going. I needed a usable explanation of why he did such a thing. I learned that he did it fairly regularly, always on a weekend, he always stayed three days, he left no place to be called . . ."

"Dr. Damery?" said poor Mathilda, her voice thin.

"I called the character Hopkins in my story. I was able to learn that he went regularly, where he went—though not specifically. I never did find the reason he went, not specifically. Though I did discover that he went often and

129

regularly. So of course I felt sure he had some good reason for going to Chicago. And I asked myself why a man of his sort would make such a trip."

"If his romantic interest really was—who you said it was—here in this city an affair could be managed—so there would be some other reason or claim upon him. Perhaps there was some problem, something he did not want his patients or his staff to know about. *I* didn't even know he disappeared so regularly. I knew he sometimes was away, but— Well, of course he's in demand for consultations, demonstrations, lectures . . ."

"But not always in Chicago. Not always for three days. Not every two months."

"The hospital would know about those absences. They do know. Even lowly little old me knows about the lectures and things. But if he didn't want the *hospital* to know about these regular trips . . . ?" She looked up questioningly.

"He seemed to keep that secret from everyone."

"Did you come up with a reason?"

"Oh, yes. Which do you want? The one I used in the book or what the reason actually was?"

She stared at him wide-eyed. Then she put her hands over her ears. "No! Don't tell me. There could have been a dozen reasons. Dermatitis on his hands—a homosexual situation . . ."

"Hey!" cried Dan. "You're really good! I should have talked to you when I was planning the story."

"And you had to have a reason to tell about in the book."

"That's right. And when even the hospital did not know

precisely where he went, or why—then when they did know, at least my explanation—they didn't want the whole thing publicized."

"And they don't now. But if you were just guessing or being logical, as you said, maybe you were just guessing about that triangle, Dan. Maybe there's no truth to any of this, except the tooth bit."

Dan shook his head. "No," he said soberly. "No, Mathilda. There was the triangle, the romance."

"Involving Dr. Damery."

"Yes, and the Sherwins. They'd been friends for a long time. He'd boarded in their home, or something."

"They lived in the same apartment house, I believe. Though that was some time ago."

"Yes. They were close friends, right up to the time of the old man's death—because, they claimed, the surgeon was in Chicago at a so-called football game."

Mathilda had stopped listening. She was thinking hard about Dr. Damery and the Sherwins. Dr. Damery she knew very well, though in the hospital, in o.r., mainly, his head covered with a cap, his shoulders bent over the table, his clever hands moving in and out, expecting an instrument and getting it. He was friendly and impersonal when met in the corridor, talking to Mathilda and Karen Butler about o.r. equipment. He was a great surgeon, and a kind, friendly man. She had never considered him as a *personal* man, in love with another man's wife . . .

In love with Helen Sherwin. Mathilda had to scrabble for her bits of knowledge of that one. She had seen her; she had seen pictures of her in the newspaper. One in particular of a slender young woman in a striped blouse,

131

plain skirt, white shoes at the end of lean brown legs, leaning on a golf club. This was among pictures of some women who sponsored or played in a society benefit tournament. Helen Sherwin and her friends had not looked much like athletes. They more closely resembled the professional beauties who leaned on the fenders of expensive automobiles in magazine ads.

Because she would have liked to look and be such a young woman, Mathilda knew the type very well, and she envied Helen Sherwin and anyone who could naturally look that way. Their skin was always smoothly tanned, their dress was always simple and elegant. And whether seen in the busy corridor of a hospital where her father-in-law was a patient, or pictured on the society page of the newspaper, these women—Helen Sherwin—always carried about them an indefinable air of poise and money, combined in equal amounts. These girls looked at home playing golf—good golf, done with spiked shoes—on the links of the ultra-exclusive country club or serving as a volunteer at St. Jerome's. Mathilda envied such young women.

"Do they still . . . ?" she asked Dan.

"Oh, I don't know. But recognized in any book, who would believe they did not? And a book had just better not start any such stories about a young woman and the famous surgeon."

Mathilda gasped. She clapped her hand over her mouth, and she ran. "Brook will kill me!" she told Dan, who followed her. "It's twenty minutes to three and I was supposed— He'll kill me! Or send me off to be enema nurse in G.I."

Chapter Seven

DR. Solley did not kill the o.r. head. When she slipped in to scrub, he glanced up at the clock. "Miss Roberts," he said coldly, and watched the clerk check off the last name on the team's list. Later he would surely speak of her tardiness.

Now, o.r. was ready. Everything, everybody was in place, the lights were on, the cool, blue-white, shadowless lights of o.r. The music came softly, autoclaves hissed, valves clicked, or purred, or pinged. People moved about. Dr. Damery came in. "All calm breaks out when Damery comes in," someone had described the way the great man worked. "You would think he had all day."

Dr. Solley had been busy, cutting through the patient's side to expose the left lung and the descending thoracic aorta. This inch-thick pipe carried the blood from the heart to the lower part of the body; if there was a rupture in the aneurysm which bloomed like a tire blister on this "pipe," the woman would die immediately.

Carefully, skillfully, the two surgeons sliced away the cheesy tissue of the aneurysm; in its place they sutured a length of knitted Dacron tubing. The technique had been developed and refined by Dr. Damery.

The procedure took two hours but, the patch completed, years had been added to the forty-eight already

133

lived by the woman on the table. This was "routine" work for Dr. Damery and his assistant. They called it patchwork surgery, this mending of diseased hearts, substituting miniature timing devices for heart pacemakers, replacing valves and diseased sections of arteries with steel and synthetics.

They worked always toward other and more astounding achievements, even while preoccupied, as they were today, with the miracles of patching and renewing which they already could do.

As disciplined, as well-trained as any member, all members, of the team, Mathilda performed her duties that day, conscious of a new awareness of what was going on around her. She saw more clearly Dr. Damery's steel-framed eyeglasses, the brightness of his alert eyes behind them, Brook's down-bent head almost touching the Chief's green cap; their masks stretched smoothly across the lower parts of their faces. More swiftly, more neatly than any tailor, one surgeon or the other plied the needles and the sutures which Mathilda or the second instrument nurse handed to them. The roller pump drove blood through the heart-lung machine, the oscilloscope recorded the cardiac activity, and, as well, reflected the o.r. scene in its glass. Mathilda and others in the room glanced regularly at this instrument to keep track of the patient's blood pressure; she wondered if others noticed the reflected scene. She never had before.

These people gathered here in o.r. to repair an artery had come into the area from various places, as had Mathilda, with various preoccupations on their minds. Perhaps only the taste of the cafeteria soup, perhaps thinking about a phone call received that morning or about a family financial crisis.

But now—her duties made her watch Dr. Damery and Dr. Solley with especial acuteness, and she particularly considered the fact that these two men could now work together as a team, completely separated from whatever private thoughts they had left outside of o.r., any personal worries about their homes and their lives.

Men were better at doing that sort of thing than were women. Because here was Mathilda—she had let herself be late, and once in o.r., she must make a real effort to do each thing precisely, alertly. The men did not need to do that. Damery's eyes, Brook's face, were intent only on the work they were doing. The doctor at the machine thought only of his valves and tubes, not of the fire there had been in his home two days ago; his hand, his eyes never faltered, his voice was crisp and clear.

It was wonderful to be able to work so. Mathilda wished that she could do it, and not need to force herself to pay attention, particularly to fasten her attention.

Because all the time she was working, a part of Mathilda's thoughts were elsewhere. Doing the job at hand, and doing it well, she was also planning what she was going to do about Dan and his book.

The surgery took two hours, and Mathilda knew there was no other case waiting. She heard Brook say he had a class of interns. Dr. Damery had departed, as usual, like a streak of lightning. The o.r. head saw the patient removed, and she turned her attention to getting things started—the instruments counted, the sponges, the linens. The o.r. would be cleaned, apparatus and instruments

135

would be readied for the next day's schedule. She talked to people, she gave orders, checked the reports, then went to the nurses' locker room and changed her o.r. gown for her uniform and cap. She reported at the desk.

Brook had better not have things lined up for her.

He did not. She checked out. She had errands, she said. She would be home after six. Was she on call?

The charge nurse looked at her owlishly, and Mathilda nodded.

"I know," she said. "I know. Once a scrub nurse, always a scrub nurse. But please don't call me! Please?"

She was off and down the hall, safely into the elevator. She sighed with relief when she reached her apartment. Still safe, she thought. Brook's class would last an hour. He would give attention to the patients in Intensive. But as soon as he could, he would seek out Mathilda and lace her down for being late that afternoon.

"Holy Moli, girl!" he would yell at her. "Where *were* you? What were you thinking of?"

What was she thinking of? What was she thinking of now?

She stripped off her uniform; she found a plain dress of lavender chambray; the chalk-soft color was becoming to her. She changed her hospital shoes for some white pumps. She ran a comb through her hair, dusted the freckles with powder, put on lipstick, consulted the telephone book for the address, grabbed her purse, and flew down the stairs again.

She thought she knew where she was going, but once out of the city itself, she stopped for gas and asked directions. Yes, she had the directions right. She only hoped she had everything else right. There were those who might think she was doing a crazy thing. She should have telephoned. What if the lady were not at home? Had Miss Fix-it considered that? No, she had not, and she would not consider it now.

She would drive as carefully as she had worked in o.r. Her mind was on other things, so she would be extra careful. Lights, directions, signals, speed . . .

She would try not to anticipate what she would say and what would be said to her.

The Sherwin home was in one of those private "places" which Mathilda admired and, she supposed, envied. There were stone gateposts, and the open leaves of wrought-iron gates. Closed at night? Probably. Thickly planted shrubbery and trees concealed the area from the main road, giving only glimpses of chimneytops, a red roof gable, the upper windows of a white stone house.

Carefully, Mathilda guided her small car through the gateposts and along the curving road. She had a house number—46. She found mailboxes and signs of a lower number—30, then 38—so she felt she was on the right road. Yes. Here was 46, with a plain, conservative mailbox. Some of the others had been ornate, or even cute.

Carefully she turned into the drive, slowing to look at the house. She wished she had taken a shower. A bath always made her feel more sure of herself. This house was a handsome thing. Low to the ground; the drive swept in a circle before the curved-canopy entrance.

"If there's a butler, I'll die!" said Mathilda, half-aloud. The house was white, its windows long and arched at the tops, curtained completely within. It was a beautiful home, serene and aloof.

Mathilda's hands were damp, and she sponged them with tissues before she got out of the car which she had pulled up beyond the front door, leaving room for Cadillacs and any other big cars which might follow her. She patted the steering wheel. "Behave yourself," she told the little car which meant so much to her, however much it might mean to the people who lived in Oak Forest.

She smoothed the skirt of her lavender dress and walked resolutely to the front door. There was a doorbell button, but there also was a grill across the door.

"I should have gone to the back door," Mathilda told herself. She didn't quite dare to think again of a butler.

She didn't need to, for Mrs. Sherwin herself opened the wide door, her head tilted inquiringly. "Yes?" she asked.

There still was the grill. Mathilda gulped.

"I—I am Miss Roberts," she said. "Mathilda Roberts. I am a nurse at St. Jerome's, and I saw you there several years ago. And today I have something I want to tell you, Mrs. Sherwin. Something I want to ask you."

She wished she could ever look as Helen Sherwin did that afternoon. Her house was cool—Mathilda could feel the water-cool air of refrigeration coming from the house's interior. Helen Sherwin's hair looked as if she had just come from the beauty parlor, or at least just risen from her dressing table. It was long hair, without a hint of curl, parted smoothly in the middle, swept back and down. The afternoon light shone upon that smooth, blonde hair. Mrs. Sherwin wore a suit—a pants suit—black—linen, perhaps, or heavy, dull silk. The jacket hung straight, with clusters of white pearl buttons, small ones, down one side of it.

138

Never buttoned, probably. But there they were—three, then three more, then three more after that. Her blouse was more like a sweater—white, silk, knitted, the turtle neck close against this woman's throat under her chin. Her skin was sun-browned and flawless. Her eyes . . . Again, no visible makeup. Mathilda nodded. This was Mrs. Sherwin as she had thought of her—rich, poised, well-groomed. Now she was waiting for Mathilda to say enough to make her open that iron grill and let her come inside.

"You don't remember me, of course," said Miss Roberts. "But I wish you would believe me when I say I have something very important to say to you. It concerns a friend of mine, and friends of yours."

She supposed she looked honest—what with her tumbled hair and those freckles. And she certainly was not being glib.

Anyway, with a faintly puzzled frown on her face, Helen Sherwin touched some spring, and the grillwork opened. "Come in, please," she said, turning to lead the way along a hall.

"A foyer!" Mathilda told herself. She was one to read house furnishing magazines. This was a good house. The floor tiled in brown and white, a bowl of oranges and lemons on a dark chest, an old mirror . . .

Helen Sherwin wore pants well; her hips were flat, and her legs long enough, her back straight.

The living room was just perfect. Spanish in feeling, which was right for the stucco, long-windowed house. Inside, those windows had creamy, sheer glass curtains, softly held back. The drapery was only a ripple of dull gold

139

satin at the top of the window's curve. The carpet was gold-colored and thick. There was a wrought-iron candelabra with short white candles. A large, perfect couch in gold-colored linen, printed with orange flowers and vines. There was a coffee table at Mathilda's knee when she sat down on the couch. The table consisted of a sheet of thick glass, supported by two carved ivory elephants—ivory-colored. They might have been carved of wood. On this table was an open book, a small wooden bowl, and a low vase into which had been crammed white daisies and orange zinnias.

There was everything in this room, but no frills, no knickknacks, no doodads.

Mrs. Sherwin too sat on the couch, turned to face her caller.

Mathilda smiled shyly. "My lavender dress clashes, doesn't it?"

"Not too much. It suits you."

"Thank you. I—I am grateful that you would see me. I should have called and asked if you would let me come. But this matter is so urgent—I think it should be cleared up right away. And only you—your family—could do that."

Mrs. Sherwin reached out her hand to touch Mathilda's wrist. "Perhaps if you would start at the beginning," she said. "I haven't the slightest idea what you are talking about."

Mathilda gazed at her. "No," she admitted. "I guess you haven't. It seems so important, I think everyone concerned must know."

"Just tell me."

So Mathilda did tell her, the words tumbling from her lips. Now and then Helen Sherwin would cough a little and ask her to go back and clear up something. "I'm hearing about this for the first time, remember. You evidently have thought about it a lot."

Mathilda could see her point. So she carefully tried to tell the thing in sequence.

She told about Dan. "He's really a nice boy," she said earnestly. "He's been around the hospital for two or three years, getting material for the news items and feature stories he does for the newspaper he works for."

"A reporter."

"Well, in a sense, yes. He covers other hospitals—health centers. City General. He's at Jerome's a lot because we are big and we are busy."

"I understand. If you'd like a drink . . ."

"No, thank you."

"Iced tea, perhaps?"

Mathilda shook her head, the red-brown curls tumbling. She brushed them back from her face. "I don't want you to give me too much of your time."

"I'm interested in knowing how this could concern me."

"Well, it does, Mrs. Sherwin. It could. You see, like most reporters, Dan tells me, he wanted to write a book. Not many of them actually do, he says, but he did. And what's more, Mrs. Sherwin, he sold it! It was going to be published. That's a wonderful thing to have happen, to anyone!"

"Yes, I imagine it would be."

"Well, it was for Dan. He was just walking on air. And

141

he explained to me that it meant much more to him than it might to other people—more than that he probably could earn his living doing what he liked to do. For it seems he comes from a family that *does* things. His mother and his two brothers have been very successful. His book's being published gave him something to equal what they have done. And that's why it would be terrible to have to give it up."

"Why should he have to? If it's been accepted . . ."

"Well," said Mathilda, "that's what anybody would think. But, you see, the publishers checked. I suppose they have to be careful. About libel, you know?"

"Yes, I do know. My husband is a lawyer."

"I know he is."

"Was the story libelous? Is it?"

"I haven't read it. Dan doesn't think it is. But of course it is about a hospital, because that's what he *knows,* you see. The publishers checked for fear he had used real names of doctors here in the city."

"I see."

"Well, he didn't. He just took a small happening—in a hospital—and he built it into a story which he made up. But when the publishers checked with the Administrator of St. Jerome's, he recognized the incident as something that had happened there. I mean, at our hospital. And it happened that the people involved—the family—had at the time threatened to sue the hospital . . ."

"For the book?"

"No, the incident. They didn't have any malpractice suit. No grounds, I mean. Just because Dr. Damery happened to be out of town . . ."

142

She saw Helen Sherwin jump, she saw her hands tighten into fists.

"Now the Administrator and the publisher had to wonder if that family would sue the publisher, and Dan, for the book he says he made up."

"From a real incident?"

"Yes. But the story itself is fiction. Though, of course, Mr. Fichter—he's the Administrator—was more concerned if the family might sue the hospital, should the book be published. And he can get pretty rough, I think. And—well—Dan agreed to withdraw the book. I think it's a dirty shame, and I hope he *can* publish it! So—"

Helen Sherwin stood up. She walked to the window and stood looking through the sheer curtains out at the lawn. "Who sent you out here, Miss Roberts?" she asked.

Mathilda's head went up in surprise. "No one sent me," she said. "I came out here on my own. I saw a young man's career about to be blasted, ruined. I thought I might help him. I thought you might want to . . ."

She watched Mrs. Sherwin. She turned away from the window, she touched a leaf of the ivy which grew from a copper bowl hung on the wall. She was thinking hard.

Finally she asked, "Does Peter—does my husband know about this book?"

"He could . . ." said Mathilda.

"I thought he might, because you came out here to tell me."

"I would have talked to him if you had not been at home."

"And you think he knows?"

"Well, *I* don't know. But he might."

143

Again Mrs. Sherwin seemed to be thinking. She came back to the couch and sat down. "Miss Roberts," she said, "I am going to be more frank than I should be, perhaps. But—are you in love with this reporter? You say his name is Dan."

"Yes. Dan Kearnes. And he's a real nice chap, Mrs. Sherwin. But—oh, no. I'm not in love with him. I am engaged to marry Brook Solley. He's a Senior Fellow, a resident doctor at St. Jerome's." She was watching Mrs. Sherwin; Brook's name seemed to mean nothing to her. "And I can tell you," she said impulsively, "if he knew I'd come out here and talked to you, he would be simply furious!"

Mrs. Sherwin smiled. "There would be no reason. I realize you are only doing what you can to help a friend. But what I *don't* see, Miss Roberts, is my connection to the whole thing. I mean, I don't understand what it is you want me to do. I don't know what I *can* do. You must have had some idea or plan . . ."

"I did," said Mathilda, speaking emphatically. "If I could go back to Dan and tell him you people wouldn't sue anybody, him, the hospital, or the publisher, if you'd realize his story is fiction . . ."

"What story, Miss Roberts?"

Mathilda stared at her. "Didn't I tell you?"

"No. Not what story the young man had used as a basis for his novel. I suppose it has some connection with us."

"Oh, yes, it does. You know—Mr. Sherwin, your father-in-law—he had his tooth pulled and—"

"Oh, dear," sighed Helen Sherwin.

"Yes, ma'am. And it was that circumstance, a man who

144

had a history of heart trouble, supported on anticoagulants, having his tooth pulled and starting to hemorrhage —that's the incident which Dan used to begin his book, but the story he developed is fiction, and he should be able to publish the book. He's told his publisher, and Mr. Fichter, that he'll withdraw it, but he wouldn't need to if your family would agree not to sue anybody."

"Mr. Sherwin died," said Helen sadly.

"Yes, and—well, that's a couple of years ago, and I was still in training, or just out of it—I don't remember—but there was talk of a lawsuit then. Of course the hospital was not to blame. The old gentleman should have told . . ."

Mrs. Sherwin put up her hand. "I remember the whole affair, Miss Roberts," she said. "It was, I suppose, a notable case in the hospital. I mean, something a writer might use."

"Yes, ma'am, it was."

She closely watched the slender blonde woman on the other end of the couch. If only she could ever be so calm, so sure of herself. Right then and there she determined that she would be a woman like Helen Sherwin.

Here she was, faced by a nervy young woman, a complete stranger, and told—threatened, really—that her family might get involved in a messy lawsuit, then asked to help another stranger—

And she was able to take the whole thing quietly, without resentment or protest of any kind. Mathilda had not mentioned Dr. Damery except right there at the beginning. And of course Helen Sherwin had not. She had never once faltered, or appeared to lose any of her bland poise, or break through the reserve which must just naturally be

145

a part of her, and which was beautiful to see.

Mathilda envied her. But all the time she knew that Tillie Roberts could never in the world be like her. She could not imagine Helen Sherwin babbling the way Mathilda did. Not any more than she could imagine her being wildly in love with a man, swept by passion high enough, and hot enough—

She guessed she could be. Dr. Damery was a grand person. It would be devastating for any woman to know that such a man loved her. Even a quiet person like Mrs. Sherwin, already married to another man, who was *not* Gordon Damery, as Mathilda's memory faintly recalled. But any affair of the heart meant a lot of things—secret plans and meetings, concealment . . .

Oh, brother! Mathilda Roberts could only guess at the complicities. Dr. Damery's reputation, his profession, would mean so much! Helen's having a husband, being rich, and high society . . .

Mathilda drew a long, shaken breath. "I hoped," she said meekly, "that we could find a way to help poor Dan."

Helen lifted her head; she too had been thinking deeply. "I wish we could, dear," she said, smiling a little. "You mentioned a release of some sort. But I'm afraid, even if we could manage that, and do it privately, a book on this subject . . . I'm afraid it just could not be published. Not ever, by anyone, and certainly not by anyone who had ever worked for and with the hospital where my father-in-law died. It would bring in so many things, dear, so many people . . ."

Mathilda sighed again and nodded. "I suppose you're right," she agreed. "I suppose it's dead. And I'm sorry I

146

bothered you. You must realize that I know nothing about these things. And the people who do know about them seem to think it just would not do."

"But you did want to help your friend."

"I think poor Dan needs help."

"Yes, it sounds as if he does. He's lucky to have such a loyal friend." She stood up. She was sorry for this girl, impulsive, loyal, also brave. It had taken bravery to come to a stranger . . .

She held her hand out to Mathilda, who thought she meant to shake hands in farewell. But Mrs. Sherwin drew that hand through her arm. "Come," she said. "I think perhaps we should both talk to my husband."

This startled Mathilda. But—well, she had jumped into these waters—she had better swim around a little.

Helen said that first she must fasten the front door grill. "We don't take chances on intruders," she apologized to Mathilda. "All sorts of people come."

Then she led her caller along a back hall into and across a large, bright family room. The furniture was white wicker, the curtains and chair cushions were of a sprightly chintz, green, pale yellow, and white, and then to what, in any other house, would have been a brick-paved patio. In the Sherwin house, this large square place was framed and enclosed by screen wire and covered with a translucent roof. Otherwise, it was a patio, complete with brick floor and a small pool where water splashed from a stone fountain and goldfish swam among water plants. There were comfortable chairs, lounges, metal tables. There was a barbecue chimney built against the house wall—and there was Peter Sherwin, who scrambled from the chaise

147

longue, surprised that his wife would bring along her caller . . .

Helen introduced Peter to Mathilda and explained quickly that Miss Roberts had brought a sticky problem to the house. "But first," she said, "we've talked so much that we are both thirsty. I am going to get us something cold to drink. Only you, Peter, would choose to sit out here where it is so warm."

She went into the house, and Peter Sherwin explained to Miss Roberts that he liked natural things. Open air rather than air conditioning . . .

Mathilda listened and looked critically at the man. He was blond, his hair seeming rather thin for his age, which could not be over forty. He was thin, his bare arms and his knobby bare knees . . .

He wore a tennis sweater and white Bermuda shorts, three-quarter sox, and white tennis shoes. He explained that he'd been jogging.

"I do it in place," he said. "Every day after I come home from the office."

Mathilda said she understood he was a lawyer.

Beyond the screen wire, the Sherwin garden was lovely. There were tall trees, expanses of lawn, bright, neat flower beds, rosebushes in bloom. She watched a pair of cardinals enjoying the spray of a sprinkler, a robin waiting to join them.

Helen returned, followed by a maid carrying a tray which contained a tall, tinkling pitcher of lemonade, glasses, a plate of crisp cookies.

Mathilda drank the lemonade thirstily and gratefully. She had indeed been thirsty! She ate one cookie and ac-

148

cepted another. And she listened while Mrs. Sherwin told her husband what "this was all about." That was what he had asked her to do.

He was certainly not a handsome man. He was too thin and too, well, serious-looking. Again she asked herself how could a woman like Helen Sherwin fall in love with, and marry, a fellow like Peter Sherwin? She even spent a half-minute wondering if folks would ask the same thing about her and Brook.

Oh, no! Brook was the big, warm, rugged type who got more handsome, more exciting, as he grew older. Full of sex appeal, and women generally recognized that quality in him. Everyone would know why Mathilda had married him—if she ever did . . . Once he discovered what she was doing this afternoon, he could have other plans.

She listened to what Helen Sherwin was telling her husband, interrupting very little. Peter sat, lips pursed, sipping his lemonade and not showing much of any feeling. When Helen paused, saying that she was warm, and stood up to take off her jacket, her husband glanced across at Mathilda. "What was it you thought I could do?" he asked.

Helen began to say something about a release. "Let Miss Roberts speak for herself!" said her husband testily. "You've interpreted enough!"

Mathilda wanted to tell him . . . She caught herself in time. "Well," she said slowly, "since your family was connected with the original event which Dan used in writing his book, and also because you are Dr. Damery's friend . . ."

Immediately she knew that she had said the wrong

149

thing. Good gracious sakes, yes! Because if there was a triangle, anyone with any sense could not expect the husband to help out his wife's . . . She shot a glance at that wife. Helen Sherwin sat as cool as her glass of lemonade, still maintaining the complete poise which Mathilda so admired.

But Peter Sherwin was not poised. Not at all! He was actually angry. He set his glass down on the table with a small crash. He glared at Mathilda. He spoke coldly. "I have not been Gordon Damery's friend since the death of my father!" he declared.

Oh, dear; oh, dear; oh, *dear!* Mathilda could feel herself wilt.

Then she set her jaw, she lifted her head. "Dr. Damery," she said spunkily, "is a perfectly wonderful man! I work with him and I know! And you should be his friend if you have a chance to be. I am sure he did and would do whatever he possibly could to help anybody! He's just that way, and you probably know it! If you had stayed being his friend, all this trouble would never have happened."

"My father . . ." Peter Sherwin attempted to interrupt.

Mathilda flapped her hand. "I don't mean that! He died, and of course I am sorry. But I'm talking about the trouble now—Dan's trouble. That's what I wish could be helped. And that's the trouble I mean would never have happened if you and Dr. Damery had stayed friends. Because there never would have been a book written. It was the talk of malpractice and lawsuits that set the ball rolling. Until now . . ." She gulped and broke off. "I'm sorry," she said. "Maybe I'd better leave." She stood up, praying that she

150

could leave without bursting into tears of frustration and embarrassment. She took her glass over to the silver tray, put it and her green linen napkin down. "Thank you very much," she said, turning to Helen. "For your hospitality and your kindness."

Helen smiled at her. "We are glad you came, Miss Roberts. I am sorry that we couldn't seem to—" She turned back to her husband. "Perhaps we could—perhaps we should all meet together and talk about this situation."

Mathilda turned eagerly. She spoke eagerly. "Meet with Dan?" she asked. "Could I bring him out?"

And there was Peter, coming up fast behind his wife. "Certainly not!" he said icily. "It would make this a personal affair, acknowledge our involvement. I should advise against any change at all. So a conference would not be productive."

He was still talking when Mathilda crossed the threshold into the house. She could find her way, and maybe get out through the front door . . .

She certainly could, because Helen was there at her shoulder. "I'm dreadfully sorry," she was saying in her low, clear voice. "I wish we could help your young man."

She didn't believe that Mathilda was not in love with Dan. She probably thought that her caller had made up Brook Solley.

"Maybe we could arrange to meet with him later. Though for now, I'm afraid . . ." She shrugged, smiled ruefully at Mathilda and opened the iron grill at the front door.

"Later" would never come. That meeting with the Sherwins and Dan and Mathilda would never have a first time.

"Thank you again," Mathilda said to Helen, and she went out to her car. If the darn thing gave her any trouble, she told herself, she would leave it right there and walk home! It might well be twenty miles, but darned if she would get into one of the Sherwin Cadillacs!

Her car started.

When she reached her apartment house and drove her car into the basement garage, she was still talking to herself, thinking of all the things she might have said, especially to that cold fish, Peter Sherwin. When she got upstairs, she was going to call Dan. She'd ask the poor fellow to come over. She would warm some frozen shrimp in butter, put them on toasted English muffins, and pour cheese souce over the top. He'd like that!

She stopped in the upper hall. Her apartment door was open—about six inches. Now how could that be? Unless someone had broken in, and—

She turned, and would have gone downstairs again in search of the custodian — or maybe the superintendent would be better. Not as big, but better . . .

"Hey, Tillie!"

She nearly fell down the last three steps. She looked up the stairwell.

"Brook?" she asked.

"Where are you going?" He was leaning over the rail.

"To get the Supe . . . Somebody broke into— Was it *you*, Brook Solley?" She began to run up the stairs again.

He gave her a hand. "It was me," he said. "But I didn't break in. You forgot to lock your door."

"Oh, I did not!"

He shrugged. "I just turned the knob and walked in. I've been waiting for nearly an hour. Where in hell have you been?"

Where had she . . .? Mathilda sighed and sat down on the couch, kicking off her shoes. "I'm bushed," she said.

"All that wine you drank last night," he diagnosed.

Last night? Had it been only last night? So much had happened . . .

She said that aloud. "So much has happened, Brook," she told him.

He sat down beside her and gathered her close. She would, she thought, just be content to sit right there forever, feeling Brook's solid warmth, smelling the faint perfume of antiseptic soap which was a part of him. She tucked her head further into the curve of his shoulder; he kissed the top of her head. "Tell Papa," he said, his voice vibrating against her cheek.

She patted his shirt front. "You have very resonant lungs," she said contentedly.

He laughed, heaving those lungs. "Now tell me . . ."

"I was going to call Dan, and — maybe he'd like to come over and eat dinner. He was so very low this noontime."

"What happened at noontime?"

She looked up at Brook's chin. "You don't know?" she asked.

"I know you took a long lunch hour, and I suspected you were with my competition."

"Oh, Brook, he is *not* your . . ."

"Okay, okay. You were late in o.r., and you skipped off right afterward."

153

"I cleaned up. You could go in there right this minute and do a pump."

"God forbid! But you had better tell me where you've been, what you've done and said and heard for the last—" He held up his wrist. "For the last six hours."

Mathilda straightened enough to look into his face. "Are you mad at me, Brook?"

"I don't know. I'll decide after you tell me about those six hours."

She lifted her own wrist. "Well," she said. "I ate some lunch—I had eveyrthing ready in surgery. I ate some lunch, and I talked to Dan Kearnes."

"Where did you see him?"

"He had come to the hospital to see Mr. Fichter. Remember? He wanted to tell me about the interview."

"And you wanted to hear."

"Well, yes, sure. Don't *you* want to know?"

"My interest can't possibly equal yours."

Mathilda bounced away from him. "Maybe it should!" she cried. "That poor fellow . . ."

"Do you ever think of me as a poor fellow, Tillie?"

She pressed her lips together. "Why do I have to go around telling everybody I am not in love with Dan!"

"I don't know. Why do you?"

She sat silent, resentful. "I only try to help a person when I feel sorry for him," she said then, wanting to defend herself. She could tell already that Brook was not going to approve of her afternoon's activities.

He jogged her elbow. "What happened in the Administrator's office?" he asked.

"Oh, Brook!" she cried. "I do feel sorry for Dan! Here

154

he'd written a book good enough to be published, and that Fichter— Do you know? He talked that poor chap into agreeing not to publish it? And here's Dan without a job —he has to send the check back—and he probably won't get a chance to sell another book."

"Does he have another one?"

"He planned to write one. But Fichter—"

"How could he stop the book?"

"He was afraid the Sherwin family would sue the hospital. That's why, after we finished in o.r.— How is the patient, by the way?"

Brook waved the interruption out of the way. "What did you do after o.r.?" he asked, his eyes shooting sparks. "What about you and the Sherwins?"

"Why, I went out there," said Mathilda reasonably. "And I asked them to give the hospital a release so Dan could publish his book and have something to show his family. They think they are so much smarter than he is . . ."

Brook's big, clean hand clamped down across her mouth. She looked up at him; his face was contorted, as if in pain.

"Oh, Tillie!" he cried. "I do love you! But—you can do the damnedest things!"

She freed herself. "I thought *somebody* had to do *something!*" she gasped. "You help people. Why can't I?"

"Did you help Dan?"

"No. Mr. Sherwin—and Mrs. Sherwin couldn't really see the injustice being done. She thought I was in love with Dan . . ."

"I do too, sometimes."

155

"That's silly."

"Well, I hope you're right." He sat hunched forward, his hands between his knees. "I don't know if it would do any good," he mused.

Mathilda watched him. He disapproved of what she had done. That one thing was sure. But—

He glanced at her. "I came here to take you out to dinner," he said. "So we'll start with that. You go freshen yourself, do whatever you girls think it's necessary to do before going on a date."

"Change my dress?"

"If it will make you feel better, but that pink thing is good enough. I'll bring you right back here after we've had our hamburger. Then I thought I'd go out to the Sherwins' myself and try to pick up the pieces left lying around after your visit."

"Oh, Brook!"

He nodded. "I don't relish the idea, but I think something needs to be done."

"I'm sorry if you think I made a mistake."

"You were thinking about Kearnes. I'm thinking only of the Chief."

"I know," she admitted. "But if I could help Dan—if I could have—Dr. Damery would be helped, too."

"Did you tell them you'd given the story to Kearnes?"

"Oh, no. I just said he was a reporter, and had got the incident, that he'd built it up—"

"And you haven't read how he built it up?"

"No . . ."

"Well, I think I'd better talk to them and explain your purpose, if I can."

156

"I explained it."

He said nothing.

She touched his shoulder. "May I go with you, Brook? Out to the Sherwins'?"

He looked at her. "If you like . . ." he said indifferently. "But get ready."

She decided not to change her "pink" dress, but she brushed her hair hard and tied it with a scarf a shade darker than the dress. She could hear Brook talking on the phone—to the hospital, she supposed. He would locate himself.

When she came out, he was putting on his jacket. She stood back and checked him over. His thick dark hair, the set of his coat collar against his throat, the knot of his tie. His coat was dark green, his slacks dull gold.

He watched her, amused.

"All right . . ." she said.

"You guess?"

She smiled at him. "You're fine," she said. "Did you locate me?"

"I did. Let's go."

They ate their dinner. Not the scampi and the orchestra of the evening before, nor the hamburgers which he had threatened. They were known in the restaurant, and served quickly, their steaks cooked as they liked them, their salads crisp and well-seasoned.

They talked of the afternoon's case, and of the heavy schedule for the next day. They talked about baseball . . . and not once did Dan's name come up, nor the Sherwins'.

157

As he paid the bill, Brook asked her if she still wanted to go with him. "I can drop you off . . ."

She shook her head. "I want to hear what *you* have to say," she told him.

His eyebrow perked up. "Let's go then."

On the drive out into the country, Brook made comments on places they passed—a new shopping center, a car stopped by the police. Mathilda said nothing. She was beginning to dread the evening.

"I asked if we might come," Brook said, as they turned between the gateposts.

"They are big shots, Doctor."

"So are we, in our own field. They couldn't do what you and I do every day."

Well, that most certainly was true.

The house was bathed in lights placed among the shrubbery. Brook's comment was that it must be old. This startled Mathilda. "It doesn't look old."

"It's magnificently maintained. But it has a dry mortar limestone foundation. Only old homes—a hundred years old, probably—have that."

The things he knew! Again Mathilda had nothing to say.

This time the front door was opened by a maid—the same maid who had brought lemonade that afternoon. Now her uniform was black, with a white apron.

She smiled and nodded to Mathilda, said, "Come in, sir," to Brook. "Mrs. Sherwin asks you to join them in the family room, sir. They are having coffee."

"They eat late," said Mathilda at Brook's shoulder.

"So did we," he reminded her.

158

As they entered the green and white family room, Helen Sherwin came to greet them. She still wore the handsome black suit. Peter had changed from shorts and sweater to white slacks and a pale blue pullover. He was not the casual type, Mathilda decided. He turned to introduce a third person, an older woman in a blue dress, the skirt long.

"My mother," he said, "Mrs. Sherwin . . ."

"So you had better think of me as Helen," said her daughter-in-law. "And I am glad to meet, at last, young Dr. Solley."

Mathilda was being introduced to Mrs. Sherwin, but she kept an ear pricked.

". . . at least," Brook was saying, "you have the name right."

"No, really," said Helen. "I've heard some flattering things about you."

He was entirely self-assured and poised, Mathilda thought with pride and some envy. Perhaps one day she would learn . . . No, she doubted if she ever would. But she would try to learn to keep her mouth shut. That was one thing she must do tonight! Beginning now!

Mrs. Sherwin, who was a distinguished-looking lady, but certainly not a pretty one, was a talker. She asked Brook what kind of doctor he was. She meant his specialty, and Brook knew that darn well, but he answered, as he accepted a cup of coffee, "I try—I want—to make sick people well."

"There!" laughed Helen. "That should hold you for a time, Miss Victoria."

By then they were all seated—Mathilda on the couch

159

with "Victoria," Peter Sherwin and Brook in big chairs, Helen on a straight-backed small chair near Brook.

Brook was saying something about their home—beautifully maintained. Had they remodeled it?

"Many times," said Peter. "My father bought this rather large estate and cut it up into acre lots; he put restrictions on things built and planted. This was all thirty or forty years ago."

"Forty," said Mrs. Sherwin. "We lived in this house for a time, but Helen has done all the beautiful things. We turned it over to the young people five years ago. It was too large for us."

"It's too large for us, too," said Helen, laughing. "But I couldn't bear to give it up to strangers."

"You don't have children," said Brook, as if announcing a fact rather than asking a question.

"No," Peter Sherwin agreed. "The world is already too largely overpopulated. You know that, Solley."

Brook nodded. "But I also know that the overpopulation is not by educated, healthy people."

Mr. Sherwin smiled—a thin, tolerant smile. "You evidently disagree with me."

"Of course I disagree. Personally, I plan on six or eight children . . ." Mathilda clapped her hand over her mouth. He did not glance her way. "I plan to raise them to have a sane and healthy conscience, a sense of obligation to the world and to humanity."

"A grain of sand on the desert floor," commented Peter Sherwin.

"Maybe," Brook agreed. "But at least it will be one grain. Your cut-off method, Mr. Sherwin, will quickly populate our world with the indolent, the chronically unhealthy, the mental problems—those people don't know or care about family limitations. They . . ."

At this point, the maid interrupted. There was, she said, a telephone call for Dr. Solley.

Brook rose, Helen Sherwin with him. "You can take it out on the porch," she said. "I'll show you."

From where they sat, Mathilda and Mrs. Sherwin could see them and hear them.

Mathilda frankly listened. She explained to Mrs. Sherwin that if Brook were called, she would be needed, too, probably. Mrs. Sherwin nodded and smiled. She wanted to ask what Mathilda did, but the younger woman put up her hand for silence.

So they listened and watched. Helen continued to stand beside the doctor under a white wicker-shaded center light. Mathilda leaned forward.

Evidently a patient had heart symptoms. The calling doctor wanted to talk to a specialist. Having contacted St. Jerome's, his call was transferred to Brook, who listened. "Try to convert," he said then. That meant the doctor should apply apparatus to induce shock. "Can you bring him into the hospital?" he asked.

Evidently the attending doctor was afraid that if he moved his patient he would die.

Brook talked to him about that. He would give detailed directions, he said, and as soon as the response was satisfactory, there would be a properly equipped ambulance available. "Now, listen," he said.

Helen started to leave, but he put his hand on her arm. "You can stay," he said. "This won't take long."

161

So she did stay, and Mathilda watched them. No longer interested in what Brook was telling that doctor with a heart case—who probably didn't even know what was meant by converting—now she was no longer a professional, but just a girl, jealous of another woman—one she thought much more attractive than she was. Brook and Helen made a wonderful picture there under the light of that wide-shaded lamp. Helen's hair shone like pale gilt on silver. She was slender, and her clothes fitted exactly. She was older—maybe about Brook's age, and intelligent—poised. She was every single thing Mathilda wished she was. And Brook—well, of course, he always looked great. He was poised, too, and sure of himself. He stood just right, his green coat fitted . . .

Now he was finished with his call back to the hospital; he smiled at Helen when he put the phone down, said something about being sorry for the interruption.

"It's quite all right," said Helen, her voice clear. "I felt right at home. My father is a doctor, too, you know."

Brook went to look through the screen at the garden. Helen turned on more lights, and they went outside, smiling, talking.

"They'll be right back," the elder Mrs. Sherwin assured Mathilda.

Was her jealousy showing? Probably. She glanced across at Peter Sherwin, who seemed completely unconcerned. He had taken up a magazine and was reading.

Mathilda smiled apologetically at Peter's mother. "We came out here to talk," she said uncertainly.

"You will . . . Oh, here they come now! I told you . . ."

162

She had, and she had been right. Helen and Brook were returning, snapping off lights as they came into the porch and crossed it to the family room. Brook had a yellow rosebud in his hand which he brought to Mathilda, then went to the chair where he had been sitting.

"I'd better be getting said what I came out here to say," he told the others. Peter closed his magazine but kept it in his hands. "Mathilda here tells me that she came out this afternoon—" Everyone looked at Mathilda, and she could feel her face getting red.

". . . and," Brook continued, "I suppose I'd better say first, to you and to her, that this whole thing must stop!"

Mrs. Sherwin, Senior, said she would like to know just what thing, specifically—

Four people were ready to tell her, but finally Brook took over. He attempted to sketch the problem of the book written, the hospital's involvement, Mathilda's good intentions. Yes, and the picture of the young man's career having collapsed . . .

Mrs. Sherwin kept interrupting with comments and proposals. She was, Mathilda decided, a very nice person, well meaning, though not too practical. She had that assured precision which marked her for a true lady. "I guess it's breeding," Mathilda told herself. "Money—being sure of her position . . ."

She looked across at Brook. He was talking well, and he too had confidence. He too was attractive, and strong, and sure of himself.

One of Mrs. Sherwin's interruptions was to ask if he had been her husband's doctor. "He had these two heart attacks, you know."

163

Brook told her that he'd been a resident for both sessions. "I knew the case," he said guardedly.

"But they were a couple of years apart, and the final one was a year ago."

"Yes, that's true. But you see, one doesn't become a surgeon overnight, Mrs. Sherwin. It takes—it took me—about five years to learn general surgery, and even longer to get where I am now in thoracic surgery."

"Added to four years' undergraduate study, and four years of medical school," said Helen Sherwin.

Brook laughed. "That's right. The training turns us doctors into old, old men!"

"I'd think you would give up the idea entirely," said Mrs. Sherwin. "I know how bored Peter used to get with his law training."

"We get bored, too," Brook agreed. "And impatient to get the thing learned, to begin practice, to earn some money so we can marry and have a family. And some do quit or decide against specialist training. That's where Dr. Damery comes into the picture. He makes the training something more than an introduction to the operating suite and rounds. He takes on his young surgeons as a personal project. I remember my first week with him. He did the usual get-acquainted things, the tours of the hospital, the labs. We listened to the expected lectures by him and other staff surgeons. Damery felt that a little social life could be added. He took us to a baseball game and gave a party for us—there were three of us going into Cardiac —and that party in his home did a lot to show us the man he was. Beyond that, he reviewed for us the things he expected us already to know, and which we did know. The

164

practices and procedures of his hospital, especially for emergency care. He did this so we could more easily become a part of his team to care for sick people in his department. We three, and the men ahead of us, all took advantage of these orientation sessions for the new men and were ready to praise the program."

"Don't all doctors . . . ?" Peter began.

"Orient their new men?" Brook took up the point. "No, sir, they don't. Generally, a new resident is thrown right into the new service and expected to know what he is doing, what he is expected to do. Dr. Damery instructs his new men; he discusses the instruments we will use, he teaches us to tie the knots he'll want. That's why, you know, it is better to train in a teaching hospital. The training in a non-teaching one is more haphazard. Dr. Damery knows what problems will come up in Cardiac and he sees to it that we are taught what to do and how to do it. I should not have been the one called on that case tonight, but Dr. Damery had given me demonstrations on the surgical techniques used in shock cases involving circulatory failure. So tonight I could tell that doctor who called for specific advice exactly what to do. Damery demonstrated his techniques on animals, and made us feel that the dog under his hands was a patient who had been in an acute auto accident. We were taught everything we would ever need to know so that when we were considered finished we would be able to work as Dr. Damery does, and to teach upcoming interns to make their morning rounds at six-thirty, put on clean dressings, get their lab work done by seven forty-five, when he must be in o.r. We were taught to ask questions, to attend the afternoon con-

165

ferences, and to attend all of them. We were taught well, so that we could, and can now, train the medical students and interns coming up behind us. And we always, always could go to Damery. His office door is never closed. I don't think it has a lock."

"In other words," drawled Peter Sherwin, "you like the man."

Brook tossed his head. "It isn't a matter of—though of course I do like him. But my point is that he is a valuable man, and he should not be touched by this tempest which threatens to blow up around him and the work he does— that he should continue doing!

"Of course I like him!"

"Because he gave a party for you at his home," said Peter Sherwin.

Mathilda looked at Brook in alarm. She had known him to blow up for less. But tonight he only shrugged.

"It showed him to be more than a machine of medicine," he said patiently, as if urging the other man to understand this point.

"We know Dr. Damery," said Mrs. Sherwin. "He once lived in an apartment which we owned. I liked him then, and even considered him good-looking."

Brook laughed. "He doesn't think he's pretty, and of course he doesn't need to be. He's a whale of a surgeon. I'm proud now to be his chief resident. I hope the training I am giving to the younger doctors is as thorough as he gave me."

"I think," said Helen, "that, in telling us about your training, you left out something important. Very important."

166

Brook glanced at her. "Oh?" he asked.

"Yes. That Dr. Damery had a—well, I don't know you well enough to call you wonderful, but certainly I can say that he had an appreciative and responsive pupil."

Mathilda stared at the young woman, her fingertips icy-cold. And a thought crept into her mind. Was Brook here—had he come here—to speak for Dr. Damery? She had thought his main concern was for her involvement, to clear up any harm which her afternoon's call might have created . . . She wanted to ask this question of Brook, but of course she could not. For one thing, he wouldn't tell her. But she did wish she knew . . .

She again listened to what was being said. "It is because he is valuable, and his work is," Brook was explaining, "that I know this tangle must be straightened out, that it is worth clearing up."

"To save Damery's hide," said Peter dryly.

"I think he need not be involved in this at all," said his mother firmly. "But I do think he should tell us just *where* he was when Mark died."

There was a long minute of ringing silence. Mathilda was ready to say something about that not being the question now, when Helen Sherwin took over. And she ignored her mother-in-law's statement entirely.

She smiled on Brook Solley. It was evident that she liked him and she was ready to take a position beside him. She was sure, she said confidently, that things could be worked out.

Mathilda, not examining her reasons, found herself resenting this confident assurance. It implied that Helen would work with Brook on the problem. Brook caught that implication, too, and he looked pleased.

For heaven's sake! Helen Sherwin was not the typical *femme fatale!* But she certainly had moved in fast on Dr. Solley.

Mrs. Sherwin was saying something about of course if the book isn't published . . .

All of Mathilda's promises to herself that she would remain silent, that she would let Brook do the talking— all this went out the window, up the chimney, evaporated into thin air. Without knowing what she was about to do or say, she found herself on her feet in the middle of the room.

"Every one of you," she cried shrilly, "every *one* is forgetting Dan!"

"Not me," said Peter firmly. "I'm not forgetting him. I want his damn book published!"

Mathilda stared at him. Brook did, and his wife, his mother.

"But," said poor Mathilda, her voice quivering, "the publishers won't do that now. After Dan called them and told them . . ."

"There are other publishers," said Peter Sherwin. "If there is some difficulty finding one, I'd be ready to give a little financial boost to the project."

Mathilda sat down. Again the room was held static in a thick, shocked silence.

Mathilda coughed a little. "I'm sorry," she apologized. "But do you mean, Mr. Sherwin, that you wouldn't have sued? If Dan had published the book, I mean."

"Sued the author? No, Miss Roberts, I would not have done that. I can't speak for the hospital, of course, or for

168

—what did you call it, Solley? Yes! The Cardiac Service. I can't speak for them, of course. But, personally, I would like to see the whole story told in public. I always did think it should be. Doctors—even the wonderful doctors—have their personal sides, their frailties, their weaknesses."

"And you are an idol breaker," said Brook Solley coldly. "Your quarrel has been, and still is, with Dr. Damery. You, through what seems to be a complete ignorance of medicine and medical procedures—" He broke off, leaving his angry words hanging in the air.

He was remembering the triangle.

Damery—Helen—and Peter.

He glanced at Mathilda, and he saw that she was remembering it, too. Did she know if that complication was told about in Kearnes's blasted book? Brook shook out a white handkerchief and mopped his face.

Mathilda looked down at her clasped hands, wondering if Brook also was finding it difficult to imagine Helen Sherwin, that poised, cool, well-groomed woman, engaged in such an affair, with passion urging her into meetings kept secret, elaborately and excitedly arranged for and accomplished. It was almost impossible to picture the details of those rendezvous, but then it was almost as impossible to imagine Helen's immaculate, ladylike person ever having been in love with Peter Sherwin.

Mathilda shook herself back into attention to what was going on in the green and white family room of the Sherwin home. Peter Sherwin was talking still, saying that, oh, yes, his quarrel definitely was with Dr. Damery.

"I understood that you were friends," said Brook.

"I used to think that he was my friend," agreed Peter.

169

"But what kind of friend were you? If you . . ."

"I was the kind who counted on a friend to stand by one, to be willing to help when needed."

"Sometimes help is not equally understood by friends. Isn't it possible that Dr. Damery would expect you to do something for him outside of what you would know to be legal possibilities? And perhaps you failed to understand the complexity of a medical problem."

"Is it too much to expect a doctor to be near his patient?" He spoke with considerable heat. "That seems simple enough for any layman to understand, and ask."

"Any man who works at any job or profession must have some sort of relief, some time off."

"Sure, sure. But doctors have built up the belief that they are indispensable, that they alone hold life in their hands."

Brook started to speak, but did not. Mathilda had things she could have said, too. That any hospital service builds teams, provides protection in case of an emergency. Dr. Damery was not the only surgeon at St. Jerome's. A surgeon had not been needed for Mark Sherwin. And even if he had been on duty, Dr. Damery sometimes lost cases . . . All these things she could have said.

She wanted Dan to be helped, but not at such a tremendous cost to the hospital and to Dr. Damery as Peter was suggesting.

She did attempt to say something of this sort, but Brook told her to let him handle this. Helen agreed. Brook was the one who would know the medical aspects of the situation. Brook said if the Administrator thought the book's publication would lessen the hospital's effectiveness . . .

Peter said the hospital should have thought about its effectiveness two or more years ago.

Mathilda spoke up to say that it would be a shame not to let Dan publish his book; there could be revisions and deletions, perhaps . . .

Helen asked if she had read the book.

Brook said, no, she had not. But she knew what it probably was about.

Mathilda said, "Yes, I do know! You were the one to tell me it was about the Sherwin case."

Peter eagerly asked her if it really *was?* If she knew that, perhaps he could get a court order . . .

Helen told him to stop talking like a lawyer.

Mrs. Sherwin kept saying that they should not quarrel. But of course they were quarreling. Fighting, in fact, with Brook lined up beside Helen, Peter allied with Mathilda.

The book should be destroyed.

The book should be published. The public then would be informed, and if anyone were hurt, they would have earned the hurt.

And, given the slightest chance, Mathilda was explaining about Dan and his family. "He got his idea for the book from something that *happened!*" she declared earnestly.

"Damn right it happened," agreed Peter Sherwin. "So I say publish that account, and if Damery gets caught—"

Mathilda did not want the Chief hurt. Though he wouldn't get hurt, she felt, if Dan had written a true story.

"What about the hospital?" Brook asked her coldly. "Do you want that hurt?"

Mathilda did not know. These smart people were getting things all twisted up for her. She simply wanted Dan to have his book and nothing said about suing him for it. Then readers would consider it only a story about imaginary people and imaginary happenings. If the Sherwins would agree to that—it was all she asked of them.

But her assertion did not solve a thing.

Their visit had accomplished nothing that she could see, except to introduce Brook to Helen Sherwin, and she knew right off that she had not needed that! He really did admire the slickly pretty woman. One could tell. Mathilda could tell. She wished she had put on a fresh dress to engage in this battle. It would have had to be the linen which she had worn for dinner with Dan last night . . . She didn't have that many clothes. But—

Last night?

Well, yes, it was only last night when he'd told her about the book, and what its publication meant to him and would mean to his family. He had shown her the check, and given up his job. Then a single telephone call had torn away all his dreams and had put Mathilda right here in the middle of this incredible fight.

Dan, the author, on one side. Dr. Damery—*of all people!* to the far side. And the hospital, St. Jerome's, that huge spread of buildings, that provider of health service to thousands and thousands of people each year, now looming bigger and bigger than ever as it confronted this group of people—St. Jerome's was in the middle of the whole mess, to which, as of this minute, there seemed to be no solution.

Mathilda, ready to accept defeat, sank into the cushions

of the couch, no longer admiring it, or the Sherwin home, or the Sherwin people.

They were not so great. They could not be human—sympathetic—understanding—

She looked up, surprised to find Brook standing before her, tall, big, holding out his hand to her. "I think we'd better get back," he said, his voice vibrating.

Mathilda nodded and scrambled to her feet. "Might as well," she agreed. She dropped the yellow rosebud on the coffee table. Brook must have picked it up, because when they walked out to his car, having "made their manners" properly to Helen and Peter Sherwin, he was threading the shortened stem through the buttonhole of his dark green coat.

"He'll probably press it," thought Mathilda bitterly, ridiculously. Of course. Or was it so . . . ?

A half-mile down the road, he stopped at a filling station to telephone the hospital. Mathilda watched him and when he returned, she asked about the emergency case.

"Nothing," he said, arranging his long legs under the wheel.

"I'm hungry," said Mathilda.

He glanced at her. "Must be tapeworm," he said. "You had a steak an hour ago."

"Closer to two hours. Besides, I'm worried. And I get hungry when I'm worried."

He had no comment for that.

"Aren't *you* worried?" she asked.

"Well, as a matter of fact, I am. For fear that legal idiot will get to your boy and talk him into publishing his damn book."

173

"It would be dangerous, do you mean? To Dan?"

"To a lot of people. Though it probably would make your boy a fortune."

Mathilda sighed. He looked down at her. "What was that about?"

"I get tired of telling you that Dan is not 'my boy.' "

"Maybe he doesn't believe that either."

"You simply cannot be jealous of him, Brook!"

"I don't intend to be."

For five minutes, she said nothing. She suspected that he watched her in the mirror. "And speaking of jealousy," she said unexpectedly, "didn't you side with Helen Sherwin tonight because you'd fallen for her?"

"You heard a loud crash?"

"I think I did. And so did her husband."

Brook made a gruff sound, but there were no words of agreement or dissent.

"Of course," said Mathilda, "you pretended to be defending Dr. Damery."

"Now, that's more like it. Though you can't have it both ways, you know, funny face."

"You mean Helen Sherwin would want to defend him, too?"

Again he only grumbled in his throat.

For three blocks, Mathilda wondered if Brook would ever actually show his admiration for Helen. If she were Damery's girl friend . . . She straightened in the car seat. "Did you . . ." she began, then hesitated. "Did Dr. Damery," she asked, "know you were going out to the Sherwins' this evening?"

174

"No!" He almost shouted, and she felt the car increase its speed.

They might be killed, but she felt better. "What," she ventured, "do you think of Peter Sherwin?"

"This wasn't my first knowledge of him," he answered readily. "He gave us some hard times when his father was in the hospital. Him and his father-in-law . . ."

Mathilda nodded. She remembered the old doctor better than she did Peter. But she guessed she may have seen him, too. Especially during the time of Mr. Sherwin's fatal illness. Since he never was a surgical case, she wouldn't have seen much of him. She glanced at Brook. He was going to say some more about Helen's husband.

She hoped he would hurry; they were only ten minutes from her apartment, and he might not come up.

"I can't figure that guy out," Brook said. "I watched him this evening. I looked at his home. I remembered him as he was when his father was in the hospital. Peter Sherwin is a man of many fears. His windows and doors are solid with alarms against break-ins and against fire. He won't get in the same airplane with his wife, or even an elevator. That came out in the hospital. He lives in constant fear of attack or accident. And yet— Tonight he offered to publish a book that he must feel sure would be controversial."

"It might not be."

"That's true, except that I believe he would deliberately make it so, that he would use it as a basis for attacking St. Jerome's and Damery. So he deliberately would involve

175

himself and his family in the messiest sort of scandal. Why?"

They reached the apartment house, and Brook parked the car.

"Maybe," said Mathilda, when they went into the apartment. Her cap was on the table, her white shoes on the rack in the tiny bathroom . . . But the place didn't look bad. Except that Brook didn't kiss her as he usually did when they were alone up here. Instead, he called the hospital.

"Maybe," said Mathilda again, when he came out to the kitchen to see what she was doing. "Cheese," she told him. "Want crackers? Or shall I toast sandwiches?"

"Do you have beer?"

"Yes, but . . ."

"I feel reckless. I'll try one."

She opened the refrigerator, took out a can and gave it to him. She would toast sandwiches. "Maybe," she began for a third time, watching the oven. Brook was seated on the brown couch. "Do you think, maybe, Peter Sherwin was trying to get his wife out of the whole complication?"

"By publishing that book?"

"I don't believe he'd really do that."

"Then it was only a threat. Under it, you think she'd probably— Yeah, that could be. And I could understand that move. I'd want you out of such a mess, too. I do want you out of it."

That was why he had gone to the Sherwins' that evening.

"You should never have got into it," he told her.

"I know it," she agreed meekly, bringing him his sand-

176

wich. "Watch it, it's hot."

She fetched her own plate, and napkins for both of them. "But now," she demurred, sitting beside Brook, "it does seem hardly fair that Dan should be the only one hurt."

He turned sharply to look at her. "Holy Moli, Tillie! He got himself into this by deciding to write such a book. There was his big mistake. Who in tarnation *should* be hurt?"

"Well, of course . . ."

"Look," said Brook. "You eat your cheese sandwich, and you be on duty on time tomorrow. Beyond that, don't have any more thoughts or ideas or impulses. D'you understand what I'm saying? I want you to step out of this affair, and to stay out of it."

Mathilda swallowed her first bite of sandwich. "You, too?" she asked, her eyes wide.

"Yes," he agreed readily. "Me, too."

He finished his beer and his sandwich. Then he said he must go, he had rounds to make. "Be on time," he said at the door as he bent to kiss her. "Be a good girl, Tillie." But he always said that.

She smiled at him and drew the rose from his lapel. "I'll see you," she said, watching him cross the hall and drop down the stairs.

The next day was a busy one. Mathilda was on time; they must set up three o.r.'s, have the heart-lung machine tested and running, the frozen blood ready. This meant four teams getting in her way. She knew the schedule—a coronary bypass, a patch graft, both times using leg

177

veins, a lung exploratory. She checked every room, scrub, even Intensive. Mrs. Bailey had been moved to a private room, with Specials. Mathilda took five minutes to look in on her.

"Feeling better?" she asked cheerily.

"Why should I be?" asked the patient gloomily.

"For that matter, why shouldn't you?"

"Spending all this money, facing more months of not being able to eat salt, not going anywhere or doing anything . . ."

"Are they sending you home?"

"I don't know. Dr. Solley thinks they could try again next week. I don't believe Dr. Damery agrees with him."

"They'll come to an agreement."

"I know they will. My nurse says you are engaged to marry Dr. Solley."

"Sure it was me?" Mathilda touched a flower in a green vase.

"My mother-in-law sent those. They went to Maternity first."

"That figures. We're good at foul-ups."

"My Special said Dr. Solley was engaged to that cute redheaded operating room nurse."

"Could have been two other girls."

"I think you're lucky. Dr. Solley is wonderful."

Mathilda smiled at her. "Sometimes he can be," she agreed. "Well, I'll see you in o.r."

"Soon?"

"Not today, maybe. We've got somebody on every table. 'By."

She had cheered the patient, and left her smiling. *That*

should please wonderful Dr. Solley.

She would tell him about her results when she went to report on the setups.

He was on the telephone when she went into his office. Mathilda sat down beside his desk and touched his bare arm with her fingertips. He grinned at her, and went on talking.

Mathilda listened, and she watched Brook's face. His nose, maybe, was a little too long, but he had beautiful eyes and dark, arched eyebrows. His mouth was good, and his hairline was fantastic. It grew in a perfect widow's peak from his high forehead. Mathilda hoped their eight children would inherit that!

". . . very kind of you, Helen," the man was saying. Mathilda stiffened.

Helen? What Helen? Did he know . . . Not *Helen Sherwin!* That early in the morning? Had he called her? He'd better watch himself. Damery would not like . . .

No, he wouldn't, but Brook had not done the calling. He was refusing an invitation.

"Nothing personal at all," he was saying. "I just don't have enough free time to attend affairs at the country club."

The country club? Mathilda could feel her eyes stretch. Yes, it probably was. Dames like Helen Sherwin belonged only to the most exclusive clubs. Dames like Helen Sherwin got "things" for successful doctors, too. Damery, and now his chief resident. With widow's peaks, and all that there.

Mathilda's face stiffened with anger. Where would such goings-on get Mrs. Sherwin with Damery? Where would

179

it get Brook? Except that he was declining the invitation . . .

He put the phone down and lifted an eyebrow at Mathilda. "Everything ready to go?" he asked, glancing at the clock.

"Everything ready. Why did you refuse that invitation?"

"Didn't want to go," he said, turning to the papers on his desk. "And I don't have time," he added, "for ladyfingers and vodka."

Mathilda laughed. "Is that what they serve at the country club?"

"Lordy, how would I know? Anyway, I don't plan to find out."

"Because you don't like ladyfingers or because you don't want to be part of another triangle?"

Oh-oh! She saw his hand tighten. She could feel the starch come into his whole person and hear it crackle in his voice.

She looked into his face and laughed. Brook was as mad as hops! Not at her. But he was realizing—as he certainly *should* realize!—just what that involvement could mean to him and Mathilda. "Go away!" he growled. "I want to finish these before scrub."

"Lunch?"

"If you go downstairs, send me a sandwich."

"I'd rather you'd go with me. We have a long o.r. session ahead of us."

"Make it a swiss cheese and ham sandwich," he said, swinging full away to face the papers on his desk.

"You should have accepted Mrs. Sherwin's invitation,"

180

said Mathilda, showing no evidence of imminent departure.

"Why?"

"Well, you might like ladyfingers. Second, you could tell me all about it. And, three, how else would you ever get to that club?"

Brook slapped one form on top of those already completed, then reached for a new one. "Getting to go to the country club is not my first aim in life," he said indifferently.

Mathilda stood up. "Do you know what your first aim is?"

He glanced at her. "Just now it's getting you out of my hair," he said firmly. "Any way I can."

She reached for the doorknob. "I'm going, I'm going! See you in o.r., Doctor."

He nodded, then turned. "No mustard!" he called after her.

"I know," she said sweetly as she closed the door.

Chapter Eight

WITHIN the hour they were working together in the humid, crowded o.r., thinking first and always of the task at hand. Trained to do the right things automatically, they still must keep their attention on the job at hand. The patient must never be forgotten; he was the factor; no matter how many hours the team had practiced doing this precise routine, he could cause a hitch, he could demand an instant and effective change in course. Hitches could happen. Two days ago this particular team had stood ready to operate on Mrs. Bailey, and the section had been aborted.

Today, so far, nothing undue was happening. A Viennese waltz was soft in the air, valves hissed, signals pinged, a man spoke, a bit of steel struck a chrome surface, someone hummed . . .

Finding two bad arteries on the bypass did not disturb them; the team was prepared to use the long vein, and had it ready for dissection . . . Dr. Solley spoke clearly, when he spoke at all. "First break, love," he said to one of the girls, "get me another pair of gloves. These seem tight around the wrists—for some reason—"

Love? Mathilda looked up at Brook. Of course, all there was to see was his green cap, his forehead faintly glistening. "Wipe," said the o.r. head automatically to "love," the circulating. Brook's eyelashes were just about as good as his widow's peak as he looked down at the patient; he was concentrated even if Miss Roberts was not. The dark lashes lay upon his cheeks, just above the band of his face mask. So, yes, that was Brook there by the table, not Dan Kearnes. Yet it was Dan who called all the girls "love," and—

"They ration pans around here," the assisting surgeon was saying, and the o.r. head snapped her attention back to where it belonged, on the job.

She kept it there, too—almost entirely, letting only smokelike wisps of attention and thought touch other matters as the long day progressed.

But it was difficult, she told herself in a quick break between cases, to forget all that had been, and was, happening. Did Brook never let his thoughts stray? To Helen Sherwin? To Dan? To Mathilda? To what had been said and done the evening before, to things Mathilda suspected had come up for him when she was not around? Had he and Damery talked very much? They must have talked some! Had Brook talked to Fichter? Even to Dan himself?

Men were so darned secretive. Clannish. They liked girls, and trusted them enough to marry them and give them babies to raise, but the best of them could take off, and did take off, into their darned little sessions with other men, only by an occasional word ever indicating that there were such meetings of the male mind and personality. Women—well, they gabbled.

"I saw Mary today, and she said . . ." That was the sort of thing they chattered about with each other and to their menfolk.

183

But men . . .

It was hard today to avoid thinking, ever so briefly, of Dan's problem. Mainly, she thought, because she was constantly seeing Dr. Damery, who had moved into position as hero-villain of the whole piece.

Not a position he had chosen for himself certainly.

But there he was . . . Just as here he was, popping into o.r. when the procedure was ready, reaching his gloved hand for an instrument, listening to Dr. Solley's terse report on the case up to that point. This was Dr. Damery's surgery, this was his o.r. When he came in, there was always a tightening of attention and posture. His great, round-lensed glasses flashed, his clever hands moved swiftly, firmly, or delicately, as required. Calm himself, he set everyone else on tiptoe. He was a super-skilled surgeon, and those who worked with him wanted to meet his expectations.

Mathilda was entirely familiar with Dr. Damery in o.r. She could anticipate his every move and judge by his hand, his shoulder, the incline of his head, how well the work was going. Brook was just about as good; he had learned to be, but Damery was the master. His judgment, his sure knife, the sutures in his clever fingers, the tidiness of an incision, opened or closed, marked him as the master. Mathilda always enjoyed seeing him work.

But today she looked at him differently. Today she saw him as a man, as Helen Sherwin's lover—and the picture, being an entirely new one, had to be studied. How did this man speak of love? How did these hands touch a woman? How did his voice change?

People—women—adored Dr. Damery. But it was as a

184

clever surgeon, placed on a pedestal by his skill, his ability to save life, to ease pain, to perform superhuman tasks of healing. Now Mathilda, in the briefest of glances, looked at him in a new role. Helen Sherwin may have "adored" him, too. But there would have to be a difference. Did her head find a warm hollow in this man's shoulder? Did this man's voice soften and deepen when he held her close? Did those skillful fingers twine themselves with Helen's?

How did they manage their times of lovemaking? His position as Chief Surgeon of Cardiovascular Diseases at St. Jerome's, her position as wife to Peter Sherwin, Attorney at Law, must require special efforts. Dr. Damery could not just drop in on Helen the way Brook did on Mathilda, tousel her hair, stroke her throat, lie on her couch with his head in her lap, listening to music . . .

Or did he? Once arranged, provided for, all lovers must do about the same things.

But Mathilda could not readily imagine Dr. Damery concerned with such maneuverings, such satisfactions. She knew almost nothing about the man whom she saw every day, at whose elbow she stood, whom she heard, as now, speaking to the pump man, politely asking Dr. Solley to "catch that bleeder down there, Doctor," even asking the circulating to get his mask-tape off his ear. Yet Gordon Damery was a man of mystery. Mathilda knew only a very few things about him, not what his amusements were, his tastes in food, in books, in friends. What he did when he rested. Where he had been, where did he go on that fatal weekend when Mark Sherwin had died and Dr. Damery could not be located? *Where did he go?*

More keenly than she had ever done before, that day

Mathilda watched Dr. Damery work. If ever her heart valve should become rigid and obstruct the flow of blood, she hoped that this man would be at hand to do as he was doing today. The patient was on the machine, Dr. Damery cut into the aorta and removed the valve. "Beautiful, beautiful," he murmured, because, as he had suspected, the valve was heavily calcified and stiff. Dr. Solley slipped the metal ring of the artificial valve into the tissue of the heart, just beneath the opening into the aorta. He twisted the ring hard, its teeth bit into the heart and held. No sutures would be needed to hold the ring and cage. Brook squeezed the plastic ball into the heart cage; the surgeons closed the incision into the aorta.

"All right, Tony," said Dr. Damery, "you can stop the pump." Here was a breathless moment for the whole team. The pump stopped, and the patient's heart began to work. It pulsed several times; then a spasmodic twitch set in. "He's fibrillating," said someone unnecessarily. The muscles of the heart were behaving erratically, not meshing as they would need to do for proper pressure.

Brook seized the two metal paddles which Mathilda had ready for him; the handles were wooden, connecting with electric cords. He thrust the paddles into the chest cavity around the heart. "Hit 'em, Joe!" he shouted to the cardiologist, who switched on the current; every eye was on the resident. Twice, twelve hundred and fifty volts slammed into the patient. Fibrillation ceased, the heart pulsed regularly and strongly. This problem was solved. Dr. Damery could hurry away, grab a sandwich, get a cola drink, then go on rounds, urgently hurrying, urgently intent. He was a great surgeon, and surely a great man.

186

Before he and Brook left this o.r., he was planning and looking forward to the surgery for the next morning.

That would be on a child—well, now a young man of eighteen, but he looked to be no more than nine, and he weighed less than a hundred pounds. He was four and a half feet tall. His heart beat so faintly that the pulse could scarcely be detected. Dr. Damery guessed that the boy's heart was in some sort of strait jacket. The next morning, he said, they would operate and find out.

For now, this patient on the table must be finished and moved to Recovery. Mathilda's girls must get things ready for the morning's work, with one o.r. left available for emergencies. The heart-lung team were busy about their own tasks. And Mathilda, her ankles aching, her back tired, still was doing some thinking.

Now about Dan . . .

The case tomorrow could turn out to be one of the sort which, typically, he could have used for one of his feature stories. He would have found out about it, hung around the corridor, the lounges and the nurses' stations until he got the hospital side of the story.

Mathilda missed Dan's bright, inquisitive person, which had become so familiar a part of the hospital scene. She wished things could go back to the way they had been just days ago. She knew that Dan must have the same wish. What was he going to do? She hoped Helen, or someone, would talk Peter Sherwin out of helping Dan to publish his book. To get into such a vindictive procedure was not the kind of thing he could handle well.

Of course she was as sorry as she could be for him. For anyone to have even a small wish seem to be granted and then melt into disappointment, Mathilda knew would be hard. But when it came to realizing one's life ambition, and then have that triumph snatched away— What would Dan do?

Could he perhaps get his old job back and start over? Mathilda wished she dared call him and tell him about tomorrow's case. But Brook would kill her! Worse, he might be done with her for the rest of time. Though, maybe, without her, Dan could get his job back, and would be prowling the hospital halls again. He would find the interesting cases for himself.

Having won his victory and squashed the book, the Administrator should be somewhat lenient when it came to granting permission to the reporter. If he did get his old job back . . .

If he did not, Mathilda really would pity the man.

She changed from her o.r. greens to a crisp white uniform, shoes and perky cap. She would report the o.r.'s ready for the next work to be done there.

As she went out of the nurses' locker room into the corridor, she saw the surgical team coming toward her, white coats over their green gowns. Dr. Damery, Dr. Solley, and Dr. Light, intent, urgent, shoulder to shoulder, in step. Two or three interns were behind them. Quite a parade, thought Mathilda, stepping to the wall to let it pass.

Answering a request order found at the desk, she next went to Mrs. Bailey's room to take out some stitches from her ankle where the leg veins had been stripped down for transfusions.

She found the patient sitting up in bed, her head elevated. There was a book at hand, but she was not reading. She smiled only faintly at Mathilda's cheery greeting and looked suspiciously at the small covered pan which the surgical nurse brought with her.

"What's that for?" she asked.

Mathilda glanced at the Special, who drew down the corners of her mouth.

So Mathilda could expect, and handle, petulance if not resistance. "When I sew," she said chattily, "I always have something handy to help me take out the sewing I've just done. I know the minute I put stitches in, some are going to be coming out!"

Mrs. Bailey relaxed. "The only stitches I have . . ." she said.

Mathilda pretended to consult her order sheet. "Honey," she said, "you could be stitched all over like a sampler. I'm supposed only to take out the ones in your ankle." She laid back a triangle of the sheet and spread.

"Why doesn't a doctor . . . ?" asked Mrs. Bailey.

"Now maybe you could ask them that," said Mathilda, uncovering her pan. "They might tell you."

"Won't you tell me?"

Mathilda took up the scissors and shook her head. "Not me. Nurses aren't supposed to know very much."

Mrs. Bailey looked around at her Special for confirmation, and Mathilda took out the first length of suture.

"I guess you won't tell me when and if they are going to try surgery again," said Mrs. Bailey.

"That's right," the busy nurse answered her. "I won't tell you because I don't know."

"You'd know if I were scheduled . . ."

189

"If you were scheduled for tomorrow, I'd know," said Mathilda.

Tomorrow they would do Damery's "stone heart." She was tempted to tell Mrs. Bailey about that case. This intelligent woman would be interested. Mathilda was also tempted to tell her about the Sherwin case, about Dan and his book—that really would interest her. She bit the tip of her tongue between her small white teeth, and said nothing.

Wrapping a light gauze dressing, she thought that the Bailey case could perhaps make another book. She knew that Dan had found the situation interesting. Not that, even if he went back to work, Mathilda would talk to him about it. She would, sometime that evening, call him and talk to him, see how he was doing, what he was doing. But she would not gossip, not even about little things—no matter how much she pitied the poor guy.

Within the half-hour she was to discover that Dan needed her pity. Indeed he did!

She sat at the chart desk, making out her report for the day. She hoped to see Brook again before she left for home, but he was in consultation over a new case, and she would leave as soon as she finished. He'd get in touch later, perhaps, unless he felt that he'd seen all he wanted to see of her during that long day. She bent her attention to the task at hand, hoping to get away within minutes. She heard the slight cough behind her, but did not look around.

"*Psst!* Tillie!"

190

Now she did turn, bracing herself against the desk edge. "Dan!" she cried.

"Me," he agreed, with a pretty good grin. "How about a cup of coffee, love?"

She shook her head, then looked down at the papers on the desk. "Let me finish here—two minutes?" she said. "Then I'll be leaving—you can go down with me. Okay?"

"Okay," he agreed.

Mathilda looked again at his face. He was all right, she thought. Smooth hair, pleasant round face—perhaps not much of a shine in his dark eyes. Perhaps his mouth was set a little grimly . . . She bent over the form in hand, finished it, signed it, gathered up all the others and put them in the proper slot of the counter.

"Let's go," she said, taking her cap from her head.

"In uniform?" he asked.

"Sure. Why not? My car's downstairs. I wear this rig around this joint."

She didn't get the grin she fished for. "I thought we could stop somewhere and talk," he said.

"Not tonight. I've had a long day, and things have piled up at home. But we can talk."

"A little," he agreed.

They walked to the elevator. "Was there something special?" she asked.

"Not really. I've spent the day trying to find a job."

She made a small sound of regret, and touched her fingers to his arm. "The newspaper . . . ?" she asked.

"No. They want no part of me. Seems I made too good a job of resigning. When was it? A year ago?"

191

"Oh, Dan, I am sorry."

"I said a few things on departing," he agreed. "But not enough to explain their refusal to discuss things. I believe —" He waited for her to precede him out of the elevator. "I believe," he said when he joined her in the corridor and walked shoulder to shoulder beside her down its length toward the tunnel which led to the parking garage, "I believe Fichter has blacklisted me. I tried to get some sort of job at a couple of hospitals. Secretary, house newspaper —nobody would talk to me. And St. Jerry's certainly wants no part of me. Personnel office wouldn't talk to me, wouldn't even give me a form of application."

"And there's only one newspaper of a size . . ." mourned Mathilda.

"That's right. But if I could discover that there had been blacklisting, I might do something. Could you find out for me, Tillie?"

She walked fifty feet before she would let herself shake her head. "I just can't, Dan," she said then.

"I wouldn't want to get you in Dutch."

"It isn't that." Though it could easily be just that. "It wouldn't do any good. I wish there were some way I could help you. I think you've had a raw deal. And of course you will find something. Maybe not in any way connected with reporting or hospitals. You could try agencies . . . Perhaps one of the big industries would have a place."

"Perhaps my family could help me," he said so gloomily that it hurt Mathilda. "All those Ph.D.'s. Did I tell you, Tillie, that my father didn't have a Ph.D? He—he died— when I was eighteen."

They reached the door.

192

"I wish I could find out about the blacklisting," said Dan, jiggling uneasily from foot to foot.

"You'd not be blacklisted in another city, Dan. Fichter couldn't do that.

"No," said Dan. "He couldn't. I suppose."

Mathilda stepped away from the door. "I could try to explain why I can't help in such a matter," she said earnestly.

"Don't bother," he said. "I understand."

She gazed at him with troubled eyes. She really must not do one thing to investigate . . . No one would be helped should she also lose her job. Brook probably would take stern measures—and the biggest argument of all—she wouldn't find out much for her efforts. But she was sorry for the guy.

So sorry that she was tempted to tell him that Peter Sherwin had said he would finance the publication of his book. Maybe Peter could and would find a job for him.

She walked a few steps away from Dan. "I'm trying to think," she explained.

She was thinking. She came back, knowing that she must not bring Peter Sherwin into this any further than he already was in it. Brook was absolutely right. She should stay out!

"Don't you have any plans at all?" she asked Dan anxiously.

"Not plans. There's the want ads and the unemployment office. They call it the *em*-ployment office." He tried to laugh. "I'll give up my apartment, of course, and sell my car . . ."

"Oh, dear. What about going to another town? That

193

might be your best move. Your newspaper surely would recommend you as a reporter. You must have clippings of your work."

"I do," he agreed. "And I might try that, though I'd hate to leave you."

"Don't be silly. I'm sure you'll think of something. You've had only a couple of days to get yourself organized."

"That's true. And I know I must do some constructive thinking, make some plans. I've tried, Tillie. I really have. But except for making three applications today, I've done very little. Somehow . . . I can't sleep, you know. I haven't slept for three nights. The first one, I was too excited at the word that my book was sold. Then I worried about Fichter's call and the interview. Last night . . . Last night was terrible, Mathilda. My head—my head is still full of wheels. I believe, if I could sleep . . ."

"Don't you have something you could take? Seconal, or something?"

He leaned against the wall. "No, I don't," he said. "If I'd go home with you . . ."

"I don't have anything there," she said. "I sleep like a horse. A baby. A kitten." She smiled up at him.

But that evening Dan Kearnes was not susceptible to her smiles. He did look bad—as he would if he had not been able to sleep for three nights—and days.

"I thought maybe you might . . ." he mumbled.

"I don't have anything that would help you," she repeated. "Let me think . . ."

"A prescription, maybe?"

"I can't write prescriptions!" And she knew better than

194

to ask Brook. He might, he might not . . . No, he wouldn't. Absolutely not! He was a resident, and while a resident, his M.D. did not allow him to prescribe for an outside patient. Mathilda knew that!

But she was sorry for Dan. Even his collar points looked dejected—wilted. "Look," she said. "I think you do need sleep. And I think the best thing I can do for you right now would be to get you something. If you'd wait here—No, you'd better wait at the snack bar. I'll get you something; you can wait there for me."

She could not, of course, get a sedative from the pharmacy shelves on Cardiac Surgery, but she could—she did—

Walking swiftly, they went back along the tunnel, into the hospital corridor, and along it to the employees' snack bar. "You wait here," said Mathilda, going away from him fast.

Dan stood watching her. Then he went over to the machine, got a cup of coffee and took it to a table.

Mathilda meanwhile was hurrying too fast to do any constructive thinking. She would get that boy a night's sleep; then he could handle his own affairs—she hoped. Beyond that, she later knew, she did not think.

The hospital pharmacy was a busy place at any time of day. Five in the evening found many patients, as well as personnel, handing prescriptions over the counter, picking up items like foot powder and hand cream. Mathilda spoke to several people she knew, she took a bottle of mouthwash and asked the clerk, who knew her, if she could get some Seconal.

"Without a prescription, you'll have to sign, Roberts."

195

"I know that."

The clerk went away, came back, and offered Mathilda the slip. She scribbled her name, as she did a dozen times a day. She paid for her purchases, took the little bottle, noting the contents and the label. She dropped it into her pocket and went back along the corridor again. Dan was waiting.

She pushed the cup of cold coffee away from him. "This you don't need," she said. She took out the bottle of little red capsules and shook it at him. "Wait until you've driven home," she instructed. Then she went off to get him a glass of milk. She'd bet he had not been eating either. Just coffee, probably some booze . . .

She thought she might do well to follow him home— but when, after he swallowed some of the milk, he asked her if she would go home with him, she shook her head. "No, I won't," she said. "Besides, you're to go to bed and get some sleep. Tomorrow I may have time to talk to you."

She did wait with him for the ten minutes it took to drink the rest of the milk. He had put the Seconal into his jacket pocket.

He talked—he was distraught, though it was Dan's way to get excited over almost anything. He talked a little wildly, again mentioning his father's death when he was eighteen.

"That's some time ago," she said indifferently. "You've been doing fine since then."

She went with him to his car and let him thank her effusively; she let him kiss her cheek. "You go home," she said, stepping back. "Tomorrow you'll feel better and can

196

start another book. Now you know you can write one."

He shook his head. "Haven't the first idea," he said.

"Oh, for heaven's sake! Write a book about what happened to your first one. You must have a lot to say on that subject."

This made him laugh, rather shrilly. "Now that might be a good idea!" he cried, starting the car. Mathilda watched him drive it out of the lot. He'd be all right. Juggling the bottle of mouthwash, she went back to the hospital, the tunnel, her car, and home.

Chapter Nine

NEXT morning early, too early, Mathilda's alarm went off, and she stirred, groaned, rubbed her hands through her hair, sat up and stared woodenly at the opposite wall of her living room. What on earth had made her think she wanted to earn her living by nursing? And then, *then,* to decide on surgical nursing! Up at dawn, on her feet all day . . .

By then she actually was on her feet, ready, though resentfully, to plug in the coffeepot, take her shower and dress.

Combing her hair, she gave a moment's thought to Dan. But of course he was still asleep. Only o.r. nurses got up at this ungodly hour!

She drank her coffee and some orange juice, put half-and-half upon a bowl of cereal; o.r. nurses didn't get fat.

In a fresh uniform, her cap in her hand, her purse and keys in her pocket, she picked up some things she would drop at the cleaner's, the linen dress and the lavender-pink one. She smiled and wondered why Brook had not called last night. Busy, of course. Within the hour she would see him.

Before leaving, she looked around the apartment. Dishes washed and draining, bathroom neat, bed made— She hated to come home to panic and disorder. She went out, down the stairs, and out to her car; she drove the familiar streets without seeing much but the signal lights. She spoke to the garage attendant without seeing him, either, and went upstairs, again giving a moment's thought to Dan. Checking in at the desk, she saw Brook's dark head at the far end of the hall. He always made his rounds early . . .

That "always" gave her a feeling of safety and comfort. She guessed the patients had the same reaction about Dr. Solley.

She had been saying a few things to the charge nurse, and as she turned away from the desk, she saw two men come out of the elevator; one of them was a hospital security guard.

Miss Roberts ducked into the nurse's locker room and quickly changed from the uniform she had put on less than an hour before to the baggy green dress, tied at the waist. She put canvas shoes on her feet, to be covered in scrub with ticking boots. She pushed her hair into a cap and went out into the restricted o.r. area. Looking back, she could see the guard talking to the charge nurse. She looked at the schedule sheet and groaned, though she had seen it the evening before.

"Don't know what I expected," she grumbled to herself; "they only add on, never take off."

She checked each o.r., exchanged quips with the pump team, spoke briefly, and pleasantly, to this nurse and that, to the orderlies with the first Gurney, to a nervous intern in scrub.

"Don't worry," she reassured him. "You'll do fine."

Well, most of them did. She kicked on the water, noting

199

the increase in activity which marked the entry of the first case to O.R. One: Muzak was playing Victor Herbert.

Out in the corridor, at the floor desk, the two men talked to the charge nurse. Was this, they asked, where the nurse, Miss Mathilda Roberts, could be found? They had been told . . .

Mrs. Morris looked up, surprised. "Didn't you see her? She checked in here only a few minutes ago."

"I don't know her, ma'am."

"Then why . . . ?"

"We got business, ma'am," said the security guard.

The second man took out a billfold and showed a badge to Mrs. Morris. He was a Police Department detective.

She looked troubled. "To see Miss Roberts?" she stammered. "Why?"

The two men looked at each other. "We have a few questions . . ."

For Mathilda? Dr. Damery was passing, and the charge nurse considered calling him over. But with three scheduled, three teams in service . . .

She shook her head at the idea. "You'll have to come back," she said. "Miss Roberts is in o.r. In the operating room."

"You could get her out, couldn't you?"

"No, I don't think so. Not just for questioning."

"But, miss . . ."

"I couldn't possibly. She'd have to break scrub. They are doing open heart surgery—"

"How long will it take?" asked the guard.

Mrs. Morris consulted the schedule sheet. "Noon," she said. "Later . . ."

This dismayed the policeman, the detective. It could not take that long!

The charge nurse shrugged. She explained that Miss Roberts was o.r. head. She explained, a little, about teams, and blood, and machines. It would have to be for something really vital to break into an operating schedule.

Again the two men consulted. The detective said he would call the station for orders.

Mrs. Morris said she could give him an outside line. The man thanked her and put in the call. Training told Mrs. Morris she should not listen, native curiosity made her want to. What on *earth* was Tillie into? But the charge nurse had to attend to a visiting doctor, one who had been in consultation with Dr. Solley and Dr. Damery—he'd been promised viewing rights for the first surgical that morning . . .

Mrs. Morris had to show him how to get to the area, and by the time she came back, the detective was ready to tell her he would wait. "But the minute Miss Roberts is free . . ." he said sternly.

"I'll tell you," Mrs. Morris agreed.

"You do that. I have to question her."

"What about?" asked the nurse.

The man wagged his finger at her. "Ah, ah!" he reminded her.

She told him where he could wait. He demurred, but she assured him that he could not wait on the surgical floor with surgery in progress. She told him about the lounge

201

where he could get coffee, and said, yes, she would send word to him when Miss Roberts was free. The guard said a word or two to support her ruling.

In the operating room, unaware of this diversion outside, things were going smoothly and a little more rapidly than it had been feared they would. The man with the "stone" heart was the first case. And Dr. Damery was lecturing as the team worked. He explained about the patient's age, his failure to grow after he was twelve years old. The faint, slow heartbeat was demonstrated, the swollen ankles and bloated abdomen were shown.

"I don't like to guess," said Dr. Damery, "but today I *am* guessing and I hope that guess is right. I hope this fellow's heart is encased in some sort of strait jacket, and that it is one which can be removed."

The operation proceeded. The chest was opened, and the heart exposed—except that it could not be exposed. Not fully. For encasing it, enclosing it, was indeed a strait jacket, a calcium shell. The first probe revealed that it was about an eighth of an inch thick. Dr. Damery tapped it lightly, then strongly. He asked for forceps, and cracked the thing, then began to remove it piece by piece, crumb by crumb.

"Hmmmn," he kept saying. "Hmmmn."

"Scar tissue," Dr. Solley told the class.

"Lots of scar tissue," the Chief Surgeon confirmed. "Calcium deposits often show up in scar tissue . . ." He chipped and cracked, and the shell was finally removed.

Dr. Damery lifted his head, searched the gallery and

202

found the admitting doctor. "Do you have his history?" he asked.

"In mind. Yes, sir."

"There was an injury?"

"Yes, sir. But that was years ago. Five or six . . ."

"Takes time to grow such a shell," said Dr. Damery dryly.

"He was struck by a baseball. In the chest."

"Under the heart," said Dr. Damery.

"That could be, sir. I didn't know the case then. He was brought to me only six months ago."

"But the injury had occurred. The shell began to form, to enclose the heart. It prevented growth. That kept this young man's heart the size of a twelve-year-old boy's, restricted circulation, starved body tissues—and of course stopped the boy's development and growth."

He took a step or two to look at the patient's head, nodded, and came back to his position.

"Will removal of the shell restore that growth?" asked Dr. Solley, loudly enough for everyone—doctor, class, team—to hear.

"He should start growing again," said Dr. Damery. "I would be greatly surprised if he should recover the time lost."

The shell was removed, the scar tissue trimmed away. The chest was closed. The team moved to O.R. Two, and the Fallot which awaited them there.

The detective waited all morning. It was nearly one o'clock when word came that he could go upstairs again

203

and talk to Miss Roberts.

Mathilda, when told that the police wanted to see her, was upset by the message. What had she done? Had her apartment caught fire? Had someone crashed into her car? Her parents . . ."

It was a genuine relief to recognize the "policeman" as the man she had seen hours ago, early that morning, when she had first gone on duty. Yes, she said, she would talk to him. What about?

She must have made a somewhat disarming figure to the detective. She still wore her scrubs, the shapeless green dress, bunched at the waist, and her canvas shoes. Her face was pale with fatigue, wisps of red-brown curls escaped from her cap. She was hungry. The team had only taken a break for lunch; they still had a patch graft to do.

The detective glanced at the charge nurse, and at two other young women behind the counter. He saw all the people who came and went in the corridor. He could, if necessary, talk to this girl here, lifting his voice as needed, but—

"Is there somewhere . . . ?" he asked.

Mathilda got the idea. If she had committed some crime, she would not want the fact spread over the whole floor. She said, "Wait a minute . . ."

She determined that Dr. Solley was with Mrs. Bailey. Surgery had gone well; everyone was pleased with the eggshell heart. But he had been somewhat nervy all morning. Upset about something? Had he known that Mathilda was involved with the police?

"Will it take long?" she asked the man, coming back to him.

"It shouldn't."

"All right. Come with me." Even a half-hour might escape Brook's attention.

In Mrs. Bailey's room, that patient guessed that Dr. Solley was uptight about something.

"I've had a long morning in surgery," he told her when she inquired.

"Did things go wrong?"

"Don't talk for a minute. I want to get some good records on that heart of yours."

She lay quietly, perhaps counting the times an electrocardiogram had been made of her heart. She watched the tall, dark surgeon as he checked all the tubes and leads attached to her body. They recorded out at the corridor desk. She understood that some of them beeped or pinged or rang if things were wrong.

She watched the doctor's face. He was not exactly a handsome man, but so strong, so kind, and usually so ready to laugh— Not that morning.

"What *is* wrong?" she asked again when he dropped his stethoscope and let it hang from the back of his neck.

"I'm not supposed to tell you what is wrong with me," he said pleasantly. "You've got things twisted. *I* ask *you* those questions."

"And you won't tell me what's wrong with you?"

He straightened and looked down at Mrs. Bailey. He liked the young woman. He hoped that he and Damery could take care of her troubles and soon send her and her husband back to their home, ready to take up the life they had known before the heart problem had come up.

205

Brook wished something as simple as heart-monitoring devices could clear up his concern about Mathilda and her involvement with Dan Kearnes and the Sherwins. If the girl would only marry him and give him the right to pass out orders, with the expectation that they would be obeyed . . . It was all nonsense, this waiting to pay off that debt. They could be married. Brook could write a check for whatever remained of the loan. They could get an apartment for the two of them. Getting married would solve a lot of his problems about Tillie. It would not take more than a quick trip to City Hall, blood tests, a ring—they could be married over the weekend. He'd be willing to crowd into Tillie's efficiency until they found something larger . . .

Eventually, of course, they would have a house. Those plans would work out. For now . . . He would lay down the law to her that night. Or maybe over lunch if she had not already gone downstairs, as she should be doing, though he hoped he would see Tillie for lunch.

He had a real need to protect the girl, and the desire, certainly. She was a trained, skilled young woman, but naive in the ways of the world. She believed in people—almost all people. That was why and how she had become involved in the Kearnes matter. That fellow . . . Oh, there was nothing sinister about Dan, or anything like it. But he had used Mathilda and he would use her now. So—Brook, who loved the girl, should protect her, give her what she wanted in life in return for her loving trust and her belief in people. She must find that she could love and believe in Brook. Last night, he knew, she had been jealous of Helen Sherwin, a clever and beautiful woman. So Mathilda was jealous . . . She could not see the woman, married to—to a sap—a colorless, ineffectual rich guy, who gave her nothing.

Of course Helen had sought—no, not *sought*—but she had accepted another man—someone like Gordon Damery, who would give her love and womanhood, and, in return, would accept those things from her—things which Brook stood ready to give and accept with Mathilda.

The doctor reached for the chart board.

"It might help to talk to me about your problem," said Mrs. Bailey. "And this isn't idle curiosity."

Brook smiled at her. "I know it isn't," he said warmly. And probably talking to her would help, though he could not do it.

So he left her room, still uptight, and with Mrs. Bailey still concerned about him.

In Brook's small office, Mathilda faced the police detective. "This is only a lunch break," she warned. "We go back into o.r. by one-thirty."

The man had the closed face acquired by years in his profession. He had, when in training, not liked having to question nice young women. This one, by her profession, was no criminal. But she could be in trouble . . .

He nodded and said that he understood that this was the nurse's lunch break; they should get through this thing quickly.

"What thing?" asked Mathilda, beginning to shiver. What had she *done?*

The detective—he said his name was McDonald. William E. The detective pushed the corridor door closed.

"Sit down, please, Miss Roberts," he said.

She sat down in Brook's chair, then realized she had been given an order.

Mr. McDonald. Sergeant? Lieutenant? Anyway, the glint in his eye acknowledged that he had given the order.

He sat down in the second chair and took out a small notebook.

"I'm supposed to be eating some lunch," said Mathilda helplessly.

"Yes, I know. I'll do this as quickly as I can. Your name is Mathilda Roberts . . ."

"I . . ."

"And you are a registered nurse, employed at St. Jerome's Hospital."

Mathilda sighed.

"Your home address is . . . ?"

"I live in the Delmar Apartments."

The detective glanced up at her; she was speaking angrily—angry to be quizzed.

"Do you know a man named Dan Kearnes?" he asked quietly.

Mathilda gasped. "Sure," she said readily. "Why?"

"Because," said Sergeant McDonald, "he was found dead this morning."

Mathilda stared at him. Her eyes got round, her face went white. Then streaks of color crept like fingers across her cheeks. "Dead?" she whispered. Not Dan! Oh, certainly not Dan!

"When?" she cried. "Who found him?"

"A maid. He had his radio on loud, someone complained, said it had been going all night . . ."

208

In that swinging apartment, who would notice? Mathilda got up from the chair, then sat down again. In that six by eight room, there was no place really to go.

"I was called about five," said Sergeant McDonald.

Mathilda leaned forward. "I don't believe it."

The detective shook his head. "It's true," he said. "I saw him. The police surgeon pronounced him dead. The maid and a friend identified him." He flipped pages in his notebook. "Dan Kearnes, white, male, age about thirty. Reporter. You know him?"

Well, of course she knew Dan! She—

"Was it . . . ?" she asked. "Did he . . . ?"

"Suicide, we think. The P.D. doctor thought from an overdose of sleeping pills. There will be an autopsy, but we are pretty sure."

Sleeping pills. Twelve red capsules. Mathilda stared, her fingers icy, a great swelling in her throat.

Staring, she watched Sergeant McDonald fish in his jacket pocket and bring out the all-too-familiar vial, last seen the evening before, the same little bottle which she had got from the pharmacy. It was empty now, though her name was on the label.

She gasped. "Would twelve Seconals kill a person?" she asked. "Would that be enough?"

"Something was enough," said the policeman dryly. "Twelve Seconals. Was that what was in this bottle?"

He wrote something down in his notebook.

"Yes," said Mathilda woodenly. "Twelve." That was what she had signed for, paid for, and given to Dan. Had she told him how many to take? She could not remember. But—wildly, she looked around the room, at Brook's pa-

209

pers and books. At the fresh white coat on the hook, at the crook-necked lamp and his desk calendar, the X-ray view box on the wall.

A dozen emotions clutched at her—anger, fear, protest —and above all, disbelief.

Disbelief that Dan could be dead. His bright voice, his light manner, his eagerness. how few days had it been since he had taken her to dinner, bought wine, danced with her, and then taken her to his apartment to show her the check for his book? Mathilda had been happy for him. He should have kept his success, kept his excitement.

But now—

And she was further engulfed by another disbelief—in her own predicament. That bottle, with her name on the label . . . She had done nothing wrong! But, yes, of course she had. Those pills were given to *her!* She should have taken them herself, not given them to that poor man, crazed with disappointment. She laughed. She laughed aloud, she laughed hysterically. And tears poured down her cheeks.

She hunted for Kleenex in Brook's desk, and finally found a box of Wipes on his crowded bookshelf. "I was fond of Dan Kearnes," she told the watchful detective. Hysterics were a part of his job! He knew how long to wait out that reaction. "He was a friend. He was around the hospital here all the time. He was fun—" Her voice dropped, her words slowed. But he should not have— Why, it actually made her mad. Angry! She knew that she should not have given in and gotten him those pills! Dan had used her, because she was a nurse, and a softy!

She wiped her eyes and looked sternly at Sergeant Mc-

210

Donald. "Do you think I murdered Dan Kearnes?" she demanded.

"Miss Roberts . . ."

"I did wrong to get that Seconal, and to give him the bottle. I made that mistake. But I am not guilty of murder, sir!"

"Miss Roberts . . ." The poor man. He must wish he had never come near the hospital, or Mathilda, or—

"Yes!" she cried. "I got the Seconal for Dan. So he could sleep. He told me that he had not slept for three nights. He had been through a terrible time. He had thought a book he had written was going to be published. He was happy and proud—excited. Anyone would be. He gave up his job on the newspaper. Then the hospital, St. Jerome's here, spoiled everything for him. His book would not be published; he couldn't get his old job back. So of course he couldn't sleep. He told me . . .

"Would only twelve capsules kill him?" she demanded again.

"It might. Something killed him. They are to do an autopsy."

"He probably did take them, all at once," said poor Mathilda. "But I didn't feed them to him. I didn't *kill* him!"

"Miss Roberts, I haven't suggested that you did."

She sat back in the chair. "I thought you were saying I murdered him."

His face still was calm, waiting. "Nothing of the kind. I came here to inquire what you might know of the circumstances which led to this man's death—to his suicide, as appears to be the cause of his death."

211

Suicide. Mathilda sobbed. "It hurts," she explained, "to think that he would—that he was in such despair."

"Of course."

"I thought I was . . ."

"I realize that you thought you were helping a friend."

Help. She repeated the word. She stood up and went to the door. "You will have to excuse me," she said with great dignity. "I have to go back to the operating room. We have another case. I am on duty, and I can't talk any more."

Detective McDonald watched her go down the hall. Her dignity was pretty wobbly.

He went out to the desk and asked who was in charge. He was directed to the surgical floor supervisor and he talked to that brisk, pleasant woman. She went to o.r. and brought Mathilda back with her. She left the shaken young woman with the detective again in Brook's tiny office, and then she got in touch with the Administrator.

"I don't really know what is going on, sir," she said. "Evidently some man was found dead this morning. He had taken an overdose of some sleeping medicine. Miss Roberts' name was on the bottle label—she's our o.r. head. And she seems reluctant to talk to the police. I thought you would want to know . . ."

Mr. Fichter hung up before she finished the sentence.

She said afterward that no one without a jet engine built in could possibly have got up to Thoracic Surgical that fast. "Of course he had a fine head of steam up."

He did. Karen Butler had ridden up in the elevator with him. "What's going on?" she asked.

But he had not answered. Karen watched him bustle

into Brook Solley's office, the Supe following. She caught a glimpse of Mathilda there.

"Oh-oh!" she said softly, going over to the floor desk, where she was told what the girls knew about the "goings-on."

She went on to the diet kitchen, glancing back at the door of the Resident's office. It must be pretty crowded in there, she thought.

It was crowded. McDonald and the nurse looking pinched and white-faced. The Superintendent was slender, but the Administrator was not. And the way he came bustling in, demanding to know just exactly what happened! He didn't exactly invite the police to come into his hospital, making inquiries. Why hadn't the sergeant come first to his office? he would like to know.

Fichter is frightened, thought Mathilda, gazing at him. She had reached a stage of numbed resignation. Dan would have liked to see Fichter so scared. Of course he was mad, too. He fairly bounced with rage.

She wondered if the detective could handle the man. One close look at his face told her that he could, probably. He just sat where he was, having shown his badge. He tapped his pencil on his little notebook and waited.

The Supe—Mrs. Becton—leaned against the closed door, watchful. It was her job to know what one of her "girls" was into, and to protect that girl's rights, if necessary. She too was interested in knowing how McDonald had reached the long arm of his law into o.r. and brought out Mathilda.

"You have a directory of employees," he pointed out.

"I asked where one M. Roberts would be working. I explained my business and was directed up here. Perfectly simple."

Yes. Personnel office. A P.D. detective . . .

"Perhaps you could explain your business to me," said Mr. Fichter in icy rage. His bald head was beaded with perspiration.

"Yes, of course I can," said Sergeant McDonald.

Mathilda leaned forward, her eyes brightening. Just how would he tell Fichter . . . ?

She watched the Administrator's face through the whole story. She saw his jaw set at the mention of Dan's name—he did not flinch to know he was dead. But the empty bottle and Mathilda's name brought out his handkerchief.

"All right, all right!" he cried, unable to take any more. He glared at the nurse. "You, I take it, are Miss Roberts," he said angrily.

"She is Cardio-Surgical head o.r. nurse," said Mrs. Becton clearly. "A fine, dedicated nurse. Dr. Damery thinks very highly of her."

"That well may be," cried the tortured Administrator. "I know only that she and this Kearnes fella are a deadly combination. They have already made trouble for St. Jerome's—trouble I fortunately detected before it became public knowledge. But now this—this scandal can be worse than his blasted book. Together, the two of them seem to have been dead set on wrecking . . ."

"Oh, shut up!" said Mathilda, her voice ringing as clear as a bell.

There was a concerted gasp. Even McDonald was taken by surprise.

Mathilda was out of her chair, confronting the Administrator at very close quarters.

"Miss Roberts," said the Supe warningly.

Mathilda glanced at her, then turned back to Fichter. "I'm sorry, Mrs. Becton," she said, "but I have to tell this man. Because he's the one who killed Dan Kearnes, if anyone did. I don't believe even he can deny that he killed Dan's book."

The Supe and the Administrator gazed at her in disbelieving shock.

McDonald rose, touched Miss Roberts' arm, and guided her back to her chair. ". . . bit hysterical," he explained to the two professionals. "She blames herself for having given the sleeping pills to Kearnes." He handed Mathilda a fresh Wipe.

"I did do wrong there . . ." said Mathilda from behind it.

At this point someone—Brook—tried to get into the office. He opened the door, but there was not room for him to get inside. Mathilda looked up at him; her agitation had tilted her green cap over one ear.

"Who's working in o.r.?" she asked.

Brook's face softened, almost in a smile. "Dr. Damery took over," he said. "Besides, it looks as if I might be needed more here."

"Somebody with a little sense is needed," she said.

"Karen got word to me," he told her. "Of course I wondered why you got taken out of o.r. Then she said you

215

needed to be taken care of."

"Well, I guess maybe I do. But, look. These people—Did you know that Dan Kearnes is dead? And this man —he's a detective—and Mr. Fichter—you know who he is . . . They're saying—well, suggesting at least—"

Brook went around Mrs. Becton and put his big, clean, antiseptic-smelling hand over Mathilda's mouth.

"Hush," he said firmly. "Don't say another word."

She struggled a little, then relaxed, laying her cheek against his bare arm. There was a slash of fresh blood on the front of his green gown. In their kind of surgery, some blood always did get on the surgeon.

"She should have a lawyer," he was explaining to the others. He smiled down on Mathilda. "How about my calling Peter Sherwin?" he asked.

This brought her straight up in the chair. "No!" she said loudly. "Never! Not if they hang me for this . . ."

Brook hugged her and shook his head at the others. "Even Mr. Fichter wouldn't hang you," he told Mathilda.

Mr. Fichter snorted and ran his finger around his shirt collar.

"It's warm," Brook agreed with him, his green eyes glinting. "And there isn't much room in here. Now, tell me, Tillie—" He glanced at Sergeant McDonald. "Miss Roberts and I are engaged to be married," he explained. "Besides, she works side by side with me in the operating room. I am Chief Surgical Resident up here. Name's Solley."

The detective nodded. "Then there was no romantic attachment . . . ?"

Mathilda leaned toward him. "I am not guilty of anything!" she said firmly. "So what difference does my romantic attachment make? And I mean it when I say I wouldn't want Mr. Sherwin for a lawyer."

"Isn't he a magistrate?" asked the detective mildly. "Besides—I'm not arresting you, Miss Roberts, or accusing you. You've already told me the nature of the pills Mr. Kearnes seems to have taken."

"Is that all you wanted to know?" Mathilda asked, her eyes round.

"It was an important item. But I will ask you to keep yourself available."

Mathilda gulped and said she'd be right there. She was recovering somewhat. The office emptied—Mr. Fichter went off with the detective, grumbling about nurses being allowed to get prescription drugs.

"P.R.N.," Mrs. Becton said clearly enough for him to hear. But she shook her head reprovingly at Miss Roberts.

Who sighed and said dispiritedly, "I know."

Brook said he'd be getting back to o.r. But Mathilda was to stay right where she was! No, they did not need her! Did she have an idea she was indispensable? "I don't think she's eaten since breafast," he told Mrs. Becton. "Could you manage something?"

She said she could, of course, and the doctor took off in long strides.

"He'll have to scrub again . . ." said Mathilda mournfully.

"He won't mind," Mrs. Becton assured her. "He's simply great, isn't he? I understand he goes on full staff the first of July."

Mathilda nodded. "Maybe he won't work so hard."

Mrs. Becton departed, and soon an aide brought Mathilda a tray. She thought she couldn't eat, with all she had to think about, but she did.

Before she knew it, she had cleaned up the tray and was tipped back in Brook's desk chair, thinking about all that had happened, when a short knock on the door was followed by Brook again, and he brought with him Helen and Peter Sherwin.

Mathilda's hands went to her hair. She must look a perfect fright. She had pulled her cap from her head; she had no comb, and what little makeup she had put on when starting the day had long since been worn away. Scrub, o.r., the long session with the police detective . . . My goodness!

While Helen Sherwin—she looked superb! Her clothes were simple. A natural linen shift; her hair drawn back with a coral and white scarf, white shoes. She must have just stepped out of her bedroom. So cool, so immaculate. As for her husband—

Mathilda glared at Brook. "I told you," she began, stuttering with rage.

Brook held up his hand. "I left o.r. and met them in the hall," he said quickly.

Helen Sherwin stepped toward Mathilda. "We heard what had happened to your young writer," she said quietly.

"We thought we might be of some help," added her husband.

Mathilda shook her head, ashamed of having "flown off the handle" again. If she could just learn to stand quietly and wait.

Brook said something about his office being small, and he closed the door into the hall. He seated Mrs. Sherwin and waited for Mathilda to sit down again. His mask hung from one ear. He probably had not sent for the Sherwins . . . Now, tired from a long day, he must give his attention to Mathilda's troubles. She was sorry and wanted to say that, but she couldn't in front of these people. She wished . . .

She turned to Mrs. Sherwin. "Did Dr. Damery tell you what had happened?" she asked bluntly.

"Tillie!" cried Brook. "I'm ashamed of you!"

"Well, that's tough," she said, getting out of the chair. She thought Dr. Damery had called Helen. And even if he hadn't— They may just have heard about Dan over the radio or the TV. They might have! But she was tired of being cooped up in this office. If surgery was over in their suite, she should be with her girls, getting the rooms ready for the next jobs. Good heavens, her problems had disrupted the whole floor!

She said this to Brook, whirling on him accusingly. "And that's not right," she insisted. "You and I—we both should be at work, right this minute. We both have postoperative things to do."

Brook put his hand on her shoulder. "You have been too emotionally upset today," he told her, "to tell a retractor from a suction pipe."

"All right! So I was emotionally upset! Certainly I was sorry. I was sorry about Dan. It's a tragedy. But I can't give my time and attention to that now. While on duty I should be able to handle emotional upsets. And I can, really. I worked all morning, didn't I? Now I'll get back

219

to work again, though I thank you, Mr. and Mrs. Sherwin, for your interest."

She couldn't make any sort of departure, because Brook stood between her and the door, and his arm kept her right where she was.

"Sit down, Mathilda," he said gently, firmly. His hand guided her gently and firmly. His hand held her down in the chair firmly.

"It was very kind of you to come," he said to the Sherwins. "If Mathilda were not still so upset, she would thank you, too. I told her earlier that she needed an attorney."

"She will have to appear at the inquest, no doubt," said Peter Sherwin.

The idea struck Mathilda like a blow from a club. She struggled to get to her feet. She had not thought about an inquest! The idea of her appearing before judges and coroners and things— She had only the vaguest idea of what an inquest was like. Would Dan's body be there? She had vague ideas of "viewing the body"—or was it the coroner's jury that did that? She already had told that McDonald fellow that she had got the bottle for Dan, that very bottle! She had said that the pills in it had been Seconal . . . there were twelve pills . . . she . . .

Brook could feel her going to pieces like an old bird's-nest, and his hand stroked her shoulder and arm, her hair.

"If I need a lawyer," said poor Mathilda hoarsely, "wouldn't—couldn't—the hospital get me one?"

Brook didn't know. Peter said the hospital surely was represented legally. He himself was a judge and did not do much private work. Then he went on for five minutes about the transfer of judges within the County Circuit Court. He may have known what he was talking about; Mathilda certainly did not, though she sat shivering and listened. Peter and someone named Whelan were being transferred from the trial division to the equity division. He never enjoyed being in the trial division; he greatly preferred the equity, or even the domestic relations . . . Some other judge had made the assignments.

Brook asked questions and made comments, just as if he had all day to discuss these matters, as if he were not needed out on the floor, in ICU, and a dozen other places. As for Mathilda . . .

She looked across at Helen Sherwin, who was sitting in the straight chair against the bookshelves. Brook's Osler and his Gray were on either side of her head. Mathilda sighed, and Helen smiled at her. "You really were in love with this boy, weren't you?" she asked, her low voice cutting across the men's talk.

"What boy?" Mathilda asked stupidly.

"The boy who wrote the book and then killed himself."

"Dan? You asked me that yesterday. But let me say, first, he was no 'boy,' Mrs. Sherwin. He was a successful feature writer for the newspaper. And he must have been thirty years old."

Mrs. Sherwin smiled. "I had the wrong impression."

"Yes, you did. And as I told you yesterday—" She broke off and looked up at Brook. "I was going to say that I was not in love with Dan. But maybe I was. I may have been. I liked him. And Brook here thought I was in love with him."

She fell silent, gazing off into space, seeing things the

221

others could not see—Dan's bright and friendly face, his greeting to everyone around when he came on the floor, "Hello, Mathilda! How are you, love?" His excitement the night he had taken Mathilda to dinner.

And now . . .

She shook herself. "Perhaps I pitied him," she said in a small voice. "Yes! That's what it was. I did pity him. He —he—" And to her dismay, she found herself weeping. Great tears rolled down her cheeks and made dark spots on her green gown. She snatched at the tissue Brook gave her and dabbed at her face, at her eyes. Her thick lashes were dark spikes, and her eyes were enormous, washed still with her tears.

"When I think," she gasped, "when I think of Dan being dead—and then of all the people who drove him to his death, I do pity him, and I get as mad as I can be at those people. Mr. Fichter, and his boss at the newspaper. And the publisher who bought his book and then wouldn't publish it. Oh, all sorts of people. He was so young. He told me about his family, and his father who died when Dan was eighteen." She looked up at Brook. "Do you suppose his father committed suicide, too?" she asked piteously.

He smoothed her hair. "Don't, Tillie," he said deeply. "Don't."

She wiped her face, then held the wadded tissue in her hand. "You thought," she began. Then she looked at Helen Sherwin. "Brook was sure Dan was in love with me."

"He was," said Brook emphatically. "I know."

Something in his tone, the sureness, the conviction, she

222

supposed, brought up her anger again. "You all make me sick!" she cried inconsequentially. She leaned over to look around Brook's bulk to Peter Sherwin. "If this mess does come to a trial, and I am there," she said, "I promise to tell Dan's whole story. I really do promise that."

"There will be no trial," said Peter Sherwin loudly.

"But you said . . ."

"I said there would be an inquest, and there will be," he said. "An inquest is an inquiry, not a trial."

"But if they think I should nót have given Dan those pills, and that I was to blame for his death—"

"Mathilda, hush!" said Brook.

"She has a point," said Peter Sherwin. "Though I think it highly unlikely that any blame will be fixed. It seems to be an out-and-out case of suicide by a man old enough to make his own decision. Experienced enough. Any other suggestion can be stopped, and most certainly will be."

Brook and Helen were ready to accept his word.

But Mathilda . . .

"How can it be stopped?" she demanded. "Can *you* do it?"

"I could, if required. A half-dozen people could step in. Chiefly Dan's family. They would be the ones to prefer charges. The State won't. But I feel sure the family won't charge anything. It seems they are prominent."

"Did they get you here?" Mathilda asked.

"Indirectly, yes, they did."

"That bunch of Ph.D.'s," said Mathilda scornfully.

Peter Sherwin smiled thinly. "It seems that Kearnes's mother is a very successful business executive. He has a brother well known in financial circles—on several

223

boards, and operative on Wall Street. There is another brother."

"He is a technical wizard," said Mathilda dryly. "They didn't expect Dan to come up to their standards. That's why publishing a book meant so much to him."

"His family didn't know about the book," said Peter. "But they do want to avoid scandal, and even as much publicity as possible."

"And they don't care about that dead boy." Mathilda spoke bitterly.

"Maybe they do, Tillie," said Brook. "You've heard only one side of the story."

"That's true," she admitted grudgingly.

"Did they contact you?" Brook asked the lawyer curiously.

"Well, indirectly," said Peter. "My wife heard about his death on the radio—" He glanced at Helen, who nodded. "And she brought a little pressure to bear. Because of yesterday, you see."

Yesterday, when lemonade had been poured on a green and white porch, and a yellow rose had been picked in a garden at night.

Mathilda gulped.

"The Kearneses," said Peter. "One of them called the newspaper where Dan had worked. They then got in touch with the court—to ask about any criminal angle, perhaps. This gave me the word, and coupled with Helen's pressure—" he cleared his throat—"on me. . . . The family," he said unhappily, "was grieved and shocked by the suicide, of course, though they did not seem surprised. It seems—I talked to a brother. It seems that Dan Kearnes

224

had attempted suicide ten or twelve years ago. Then he had not been accepted for law school by his university. The brother said he was not able to accept failure. He was in analysis for a couple of years. But he had been all right since—or seemed to be."

Peter cleared his throat again, and shifted his weight from one foot to the other. "About the book," he said, "the publishers, the hospital here—and others—do not want that talked about. If there were reasons not to publish it, those reasons are even stronger now."

"And then there is Dr. Damery," said Mathilda, as if she were plucking the name out of the air.

Both Helen and Brook protested this. There was no need to bring a man of his prestige into the sorry affair—no reason at all. His usefulness as the great surgeon Mathilda, of all people, should know him to be. . . . That should be protected.

Mathilda looked at Peter Sherwin. "Yesterday you said . . ." she began.

"Yes. I did say that I would like to see the book published. And I would have thought that now Dr. Solley might want the same thing, that he would help me."

"Well, I won't," said Brook. "If anyone needs help now, it is Mathilda here. And I want to help her. If you, Judge Sherwin, or anyone else lets this thing get into court, if it promises to become a fight of any sort, one that would involve her, I'd do as she has promised to do. I would stand ready with testimony, in court, or in the newspaper —wherever the truth needs to be known."

"You would sacrifice your career?" asked Helen. "I understand it promises to be a brilliant one."

225

Mathilda looked down at her hands, tightly clasped together. Brook was protecting Dr. Damery. She knew that he was. And threatening Judge Sherwin that way . . .

Now Brook was saying that he could not see why he shouldn't be ready to help Mathilda in any way he could. "When a man loves a woman as I do Mathilda, he cannot let her be hurt for lack of the truth being known."

Yes, he was protecting Damery. He . . .

The knock on the door sounded very loud. Everyone jumped. They had not expected to be interrupted.

It was an orderly. The Administrator, he said—Mr. Fichter—would like a conference. Would Dr. Solley, Miss Roberts, and their attorney . . . ?

"Why didn't he phone?" asked Mathilda.

Brook was helping her out of the chair. "You come along," he told Helen Sherwin.

They made a strange parade as they left his office and went along the corridor to the elevator. The tall doctor in his shapeless o.r. suit and green gown, his mask still dangling against his shoulder.

The nurse, in equally shapeless green, close at his side.

The smartly attractive blonde woman in creamy linen, and the slender, quick-moving man in gray slacks and dark sports coat.

Eyes followed them—many eyes.

Chapter Ten

THE conference was of some length. It was almost six o'clock when Brook and Mathilda came upstairs again. And about the first person they met was Dr. Damery. He was smiling, his eyeglasses sparkling. "Is everything settled?" he asked.

"Well, we certainly hope so!" said Mathilda, going past him toward the surgery suite. She would check the o.r.'s against the next day's schedule. And change her clothes, and eat some supper, and go home, and—

She did change, and came out meaning to find Brook and ask him—

He was waiting for her, already changed into whites. "Is an o.r. ready?" he asked her.

Mathilda nodded, her mouth a bit grim. "Always, Doctor," she told him. "Always."

"Good! We'll get something to eat. We are operating."

"I saw the schedules. Why are we operating at ten tonight?"

"Are you ready?"

"I answered that once."

"So you did. All right. I'll make rounds and meet you out here."

She nodded. "I'll wait."

They had talking to do together. Not in front of the

Sherwins, or that detective, or Mr. Fichter. She might have left the hospital for a couple of hours. But she would wait and eat dinner with Brook. He'd had a hard day, too.

She helped the heart-lung team set up the pump with fresh blood and restrained herself from asking them why they were doing surgery at ten.

But she would ask Brook, and this time get a reply.

She found Brook waiting for her in the anteroom of the darkened surgery suite. He snapped on the room's light and said they would go straight down for their dinner "before anything else comes up."

Perversely, Mathilda said she would first go to see Mrs. Bailey. "I'd hoped we were going to operate on *her,*" she said.

"No, we are not. I've had her moved down to Intermediate, and I want my dinner. If you expect to eat with me . . ."

She did expect to, and she was hungry. It seemed a very long time since that lunch tray in Brook's office.

On their way to the cafeteria, they met and had to speak to a half dozen people. Dr. Perry and Dr. Light would have held Brook in conversation. Perry even asked if he hadn't seen "that Sherwin fellow" in the hall earlier that day.

Brook said that he had, and asked to be excused.

"I thought he had us on his blacklist," Perry insisted.

"I think he does. But a wife can be a powerful force, Perry."

"Oh, Lord, yes!" agreed the other heart man. And Brook and Mathilda escaped into the elevator.

"Wasn't he . . . ?" Mathilda asked.

228

"He was," said Brook. "Mark Sherwin's doctor of record. The Sherwins gave him a very rough time. What are you going to eat?"

"Everything in sight," said Mathilda.

"You'll pay your own tab then," Brook warned, holding the door for her.

"I expect to," she said, ducking under his arm.

She spoke to a nurse and greeted the woman behind the counter, then she carried her well-filled tray to a nearby table. They had a choice, the hour being late.

Brook brought an even heavier tray. "I didn't get any lunch," he explained. "I'm going back for ice cream."

"Why don't we get fat?" asked Mathilda, laughing.

"I probably shall, once I go on staff."

"July first?"

"Yes. I want to talk about that."

Mathilda drained her glass of tomato juice. "First, tell me why we are operating tonight. The team and all of us. It doesn't sound like an emergency."

"It seems to be one for the Chief. He thinks the patient shouldn't wait until Monday."

"And . . . ?"

"Damery plans to be away for a few days." And in that hospital what Damery wanted, Damery got.

"Did this come up suddenly?"

Brook concentrated on his hot roast beef sandwich. Mathilda looked at him, remembering how he had been sitting in the anteroom before the lighted view box, examining X-rays, taking them, one by one, from a great stack of Manila envelopes. Heart cases accumulated dozens of the things. He had been refreshing his mind about the

229

upcoming patient—his present condition as well as the progress of his arteries for the past ten years. Brook was a very thorough man.

Now, feeling Mathilda's eyes on him, he said grudgingly, "This may have come up suddenly."

"The trip, you mean. Where is he going?"

"Oh, Mathilda . . ."

She waited.

"He said he was going fishing."

"Does he fish?"

Brook looked and sounded exasperated. "I don't know!" he cried. "But why not?"

"Didn't he tell you where he was going fishing?"

Brook laid down his fork and his knife. "What is all this?" he demanded. *"What? Where? When?"*

"I was thinking of his supposed trip to Chicago when Mr. Sherwin's father . . ."

Brook smiled at her. "You're a smart girl, Tillie," he said.

"Of course. So tell me."

"I came down here hoping to talk of other things."

"What other things?"

"Well, now I'm not sure I want to tell them to such a smart girl."

She examined her hamburger and bun. The meat was thick and richly brown. She could wait. Brook would tell her.

He did. "I've decided," he said, "that you and I should be married right away."

"How right away?" She lifted the bun and the hamburger.

230

"Tomorrow?"

"That isn't possible. Besides, what's your hurry?"

"We can make it by next week, can't we?"

She swallowed the first bite. "By next week, maybe," she agreed, taking another bite.

Brook leaned toward her. "You will?" he asked.

She nodded. "Maybe."

"Your mouth's full."

Her pretty eyes smiled at him. "You're so romantic," she said, her mouth still full.

He stretched his hand to her. "I'll make the arrangements. I know of an apartment we can get. One of the internes is leaving. Can we make do with your place until he does?"

"Sure."

He leaned back in his chair. "If I'd known it would be this easy," he said, "I'd have started this a year ago."

"Eat your dinner. It wouldn't have been this easy a year ago."

"Because you were in debt."

"That's right," she agreed airily. "And I still am."

"How much are you in debt?" He watched her face closely.

"Oh, it's down to two hundred, I think. But I thought you knew that. You were talking about it just a day or two ago."

"I didn't know the exact amount. I supposed it was more." He leaned toward her. "Do you mean you've been holding out on me for a lousy two hundred bucks? Why, Tillie, you could have paid that off yourself. You earn good money!"

"I know," she agreed. "And I have been paying it off, at fifty a month. But I still owe two hundred. And in four months . . ."

He laughed. "Well, I think we'll do it in four days, young lady!"

"Yes," she said. "Now we will. Since there has been this change."

He looked at her warily. "What change?"

She laid down the bun and wiped her fingers. "Well," she said, "there certainly has been one. "Now, in view of those six or eight children . . ."

He laughed. "We'll start with one."

She nodded. "Yes, we will. And then—Now I think I need you to take care of me."

He smiled widely. "I think the same thing!" he said heartily. "But I thought that a year ago, too."

"I didn't."

He laughed and picked up his fork. "That's a change, all right," he agreed.

"We'll need blood tests," said Mathilda. "License application."

"And a preacher. The chaplain here will do it."

"All right."

"And a ring. Maybe we can both get some time off tomorrow."

"I hope so. I want to go to Dan's funeral, whenever it is."

"Mathilda!" he cried. "You can't do that!"

"Why not?"

"Look, if you meant that about my taking care of you — Believe me, you cannot go to his funeral. For one thing, it probably won't be here in this city."

"Wherever it is, I want to go. I feel that I must talk to his family. I have to tell them that he was *not* a failure! That he had *everything* going for him! I believe this was an accident. He knew he could have written another book. He could have got a job in another city! He—could—" She gulped, and wept.

Brook handed her a paper napkin, and waited. Then he shook his head at her. "You can't go," he said firmly.

"Why not?" asked Mathilda.

"It would be better if you did not. There will be gossip enough later on. It's better if there is no 'she said' to quote."

Mathilda thought about this while she ate her salad. "Will there be gossip, really?" she asked.

"Of course there will be. It's a natural thing."

"Is that why you want us to get married?"

He looked at her.

She blushed and said she was sorry.

"All right. Though being married to me will somewhat protect you from talk."

"Here in the hospital. Yes, it will."

He stood up. "I'm getting some more coffee. And some of that spaghetti. Want anything?"

"Spaghetti, and another glass of milk."

"You'll fall asleep between instruments."

"You'll yell at me and wake me up."

She watched him walk across the room; her eyes were tender. The man she would marry was a heart surgeon, was a top performer in the medical circus. Brook qualified. He was a bold, brave, sure man, trained by Gordon Damery, and like him, compassionate, never one to sacrifice humanity for longevity. The hospital people knew this. Dr. Solley, like Dr. Damery, was loved and respected. Mathilda knew these things, so she loved and trusted the man.

He returned with the spaghetti and two saucers of cubed fresh pineapple. "Oh, good!" she said. "You know? I've been thinking."

"Fine. What about?"

"I've been thinking that I wish Helen Sherwin would divorce Peter the judge and marry Dr. Damery."

He stacked their used dishes on the tray and set it over on another table.

"They are nice people," Mathilda assured him.

"Yes, they are. But they can't marry each other. Not even with a divorce from the judge."

"Why not?"

"This spaghetti is good. You've been asking a lot of questions about Damery. I am joining him in his practice, you know."

"I knew you would. Which question are you going to answer?"

"You'll have to keep his secret, too."

"I will. Once I'm married to a doctor, I won't be able to gabble so much."

"There are three days to wait . . ."

She laughed. The spaghetti was good. "What is his secret?" she asked.

"That he cannot ask his wife for a divorce."

"That . . ." Mathilda stared at Brook. "Damery's *married?*" she cried.

234

"Shhhh."

Mathilda glanced around her. "But I thought . . ."

"You thought what everybody else has been thinking—
that he is a busy bachelor, eligible to every dame that
comes along. He's not. He hasn't been. He has been married since he was an intern. Now, and for the past fifteen
years, his wife has been a helpless invalid, largely coma-
tose. She has suffered a series of aneurysms in the brain.
Inoperable."

Mathilda put her hands to her cheeks. "I can't believe
it! What a terrible thing!"

"Yes, Of course it is terrible. A tragedy."

"But a man as famous as Dr. Damery . . ."

"It's been a very well-kept secret. I myself do not know
how he has endured a burden like that, considering the
work he does. It would ruin most any man's ability to
work at all, let alone do his work in the vascularization of
other people, unable to help this young woman . . ."

"The worry, the grief. Of course it's terrible for her, too,
Brook!" Mathilda's face was white and strained with the
genuine sorrow she was feeling.

"It is terrible for her," Brook agreed. "Though she is
protected by unconsciousness—which, lasting for fifteen
years, is bad enough, God knows. It is terrible for Damery, to have to live and work . . . This thing has certainly
brought tragedy to three people, even to four, if you in-
clude Peter Sherwin."

"He knows about his wife's relationship to Dr. Damery?"

"A man would have to know!"

"Yes, I suppose he would. And if Helen does love him

235

—Dr. Damery, I mean—this has been awful for her. She doesn't show it. I hope they are together often."

Brook smiled at her. "I don't know one thing about that," he said. "But people, generally, believe that he and Helen have had an affair."

"Still?"

"I don't know. Perhaps . . ."

"How long have you known about Damery's wife?"

"Not long. Only a few days. I am sure he told me about it because of your involvement in this thing with Kearnes and the Sherwins and the hospital."

Mathilda stared at him. "Because of *my* involvement . . . ? You mean, he thought about *me?*"

"And me."

She looked ready to dissolve, in tears again perhaps, or in some way. Brook's hand lay upon her forearm, warm, strong. "Easy does it," he warned.

Mathilda nodded. She took up her glass of water and drank from it. "He's a—a dear man!" she gasped.

"Yes. He's a great guy. A very great one."

Mathilda's bronze eyebrows drew together. She pushed the remaining spaghetti around on her plate. "His wife," she said slowly, "was why he went to Chicago—the time when Mr. Sherwin became ill and died."

"Yes. He goes there regularly. Today, I think some sort of message had come. He just said he'd have to leave on the early flight tomorrow. So we are operating tonight."

"I hope . . ."

"Shhh."

"Don't you suppose, when he gets such a message, that *he* hopes . . . ?"

236

"He wouldn't speak of that hope."

"I'm sorry."

"Okay."

"Why does he keep her in Chicago?" Mathilda asked, her face still troubled. "Why not bring her here?"

"He explained that when he talked to me. He said he thought there were things I should know. When the matter of Dan's book and the Sherwins came up."

"Did Helen tell him I'd gone out there?"

"She may have. He talked to me only about himself and his wife. He was giving me background which he thought I might need and could pass on to you if necessary."

"Yes."

"He told me why he kept his wife in Chicago, while he came here to work and live."

Mathilda waited, wanting to touch Brook in some loving and comforting way. But the score of people in the cafeteria would be watching Dr. Solley and his girl. They knew that he was the upcoming star in their hospital world; he would work with Damery, and probably, someday, succeed him. And a really good cardiovascular man was a star to watch.

So she stayed demurely attentive and listening.

"In Chicago was where it happened," Brook was telling her. "I think he was in his second year as resident. And his wife—they'd been married when he was an intern. I told you that?"

"Yes."

"Well, she was stricken—and he must have put in a couple of bad years, with her illness, and the eventual knowledge that she could not get well. I suppose every-

237

thing was tried. He said only that she was young and strong—but helpless. And someone—probably his chief of service—told him that he would need to get away from the closeness to her and her condition. That must have been quite a session. But I can imagine Damery himself now giving that sort of advice to a doctor in training and inflicted with the same sort of tragedy."

"He'd be right . . ."

"Of course he would be right, hard as it was. She could not be helped. And to work elsewhere would be his only chance to do the good work he was capable of doing. He must have been one whale of a resident. So when his chief, or whoever it was, advised him to make a whole new life for himself, he did it."

Mathilda closed her eyes, trying to picture that scene of a dozen years ago. A younger Dr. Damery—perhaps his glasses were not so big-lensed then; certainly he would not have been able to flash his well-known, kindly smile. Were they in the chief's office? In scrub? A conference in a corner of the doctors' lounge or bullpen?

But the chief surgeon would have talked to his young co-worker, and perhaps at a sacrifice of the young man's talent and ability, he had earnestly advised his young protegée.

"You don't think leaving the vicinity will lighten the load," he would have said. "But it will, in time. Make yourself a home in the new place, make friends. Do good work for others."

So Dr. Damery had come to St. Jerome's, and he had done all the things advised. He had even fallen in love . . .

238

Mathilda looked up earnestly at Brook. "I feel like crying," she said soberly. "To think I let myself be jealous of Helen Sherwin."

Brook nodded. "Yes, you were jealous."

"She—she seemed so much better for you than I will ever be, Brook."

He shrugged. "That's a matter of taste."

Mathilda found a very small, a very faint smile. "She would be," she repeated. "She has an—elegance, a calm sureness that I will never have. My hair flies around, and I speak out too quickly, too heedlessly."

Brook sipped his cold coffee and made a face. "I don't think my taste is all that bad," he drawled.

"But, really, Brook," Mathilda persisted. "She is a lovely person. And to think of her married to that—that frozen Charlotte!"

His eyes widened. "A frozen Charlotte?" he asked. "What's that?"

"Oh, it's a doll—a tiny china doll. My mother has some. She says she used to buy them at the candy store for a penny. They are stone white—china, but not glazed—molded into the forms of children—about two inches tall. No color to them. She says she used to dress hers with scraps of cloth. She liked them, but I never did. And I think Peter Sherwin is like that—cold, hard, colorless—molded to be like a man, but—"

Brook shook his head. "You are really something," he said.

"That's why I feel like crying. To think she—Helen Sherwin—is in love with Dr. Damery—and that he loves her. But she can't become his wife and ever have his

239

children. Why, Brook, I don't have one single reason to be jealous of her!"

"I know. That's what I told you."

"Yes, you did." She sat thoughtful. "I'm thinking of Dr. Damery now," she said when he came back with the hot coffee he'd gone to fetch. "His chief advised him to make a new life, and he did. He certainly did! He set himself up as a bachelor, wedded to his profession. And yet he was married . . ."

"It wasn't very much of a marriage."

"I know it wasn't. I know it isn't. And of course he couldn't go around telling folks about his wife. Did—does Helen know about her?"

"Well, he didn't discuss his affair with her when he talked to me. I suspect that he guessed I knew about it. Perhaps she has not known. Her being married would be reason enough that the relationship had to be only an affair. I imagine they have enjoyed it. They are the same sort of people. Perhaps some of his trips are with her."

"I hope so. They both deserve it."

Brook chuckled and looked at his watch. "Somehow I don't believe that Peter has known about their affair," he said. "The thing built up slowly, I think. The three of them were friends. At one time, Damery lived in the same apartment house with them. They were friends when I first went on Damery's service. He'd join them for golf, and I'd overhear telephone conversations. He'd leave word that he could be reached at the Sherwin home. And I suppose, perhaps against his wishes, or Helen's, the thing developed. Then—the father's death set Peter off. If he'd known there was an affair, he'd have been very nasty about it."

240

"He still could be. Is it still going on?"

"I don't know, Tillie."

"I hope so. It's a lot better than having nothing in the way of love and life. And Dr. Damery certainly has done some wonderful work, Brook. If his chief was right, and he couldn't have worked well staying so close to his poor invalid wife . . ."

"I don't think he's ashamed of her, Mathilda."

"He has no reason to be! But he's saved himself all the discussion, and pity, and morbid curiosity . . ."

"That's right. He came here wanting to work, and here he could work. He did. Think of the techniques he has developed. And the great amount of work he has done! I'll bet his chief has been proud of him."

"Is he still alive and active?"

"I haven't the slightest idea. But if he is, he should know that his advice was good. Damery came here, and keeping silent let him keep his privacy."

"His private life has been almost a mystery," said Mathilda.

"Oh . . ."

"Yes, it has been. Among the women he works with, it has."

"I suppose. But it protected him. As a bachelor, he was able to do the things he wanted to do. Few questions were asked."

"Well, at least not of him. Not directly. But I'll bet his matchmaking friends chased him."

"I imagine they did. But he handled the situation, maybe he even enjoyed it."

"Until he found himself in love with Helen Sherwin."

"Yes. And that would have upset all his calculations. He had let himself see a lot of the Sherwins. He thought he was safe with those close friends. And he must have let his guard down. I imagine he had some bad hours, or months. Guilt about his wife, whom he once had loved."

"And yet he wanted to express his love for Helen, fulfill it. It didn't mean disloyalty, Brook. He was older, he'd had no marriage for years . . ."

"I'm not criticizing. Dear Lord, no! But I'll bet Gordon Damery did some heavy self-condemning."

"Until he decided that this love was entirely a different thing from what he'd had, and remembered, with the girl in Chicago."

"It must have worked out for him some way. He's an honest man. He couldn't divorce his vegetable wife, and the affair with Helen developed. It probably was a good experience. It may still be going on, and still be a good thing for both of them."

"Do *you* think having it was better, Brook? For both of them?"

Brook drained his coffee cup. "I don't know what is *better,* Mathilda. I just know what happened. The trouble is—Damery and Helen and you and I and the woman behind the meat counter over there—we're all human, we just about have to take life as it comes to us, and make our decisions as they come up.

"Knowing the man Damery is, I feel sure he did not readily or quickly act upon his attraction to his friend's wife. He would have gravely considered that friendship, and I am sure his conscience spoke up very loudly in behalf of his invalid wife.

242

"Now drink your coffee. I should be upstairs. A dollar says I'll have to make rounds with Damery before we scrub."

Mathilda nodded and made a small sound of sympathy. Rounds with Dr. Damery could cover this whole building, and Brook already had had a long, exhausting day.

She finished her pineapple, still musing about all the things he had said to her that evening—all the things that had happened that day. And working back— She looked up.

"Do you suppose," she asked, "do you suppose Dan knew and used the story about Damery and his wife in his book?"

"Don't you know?"

"Of course I don't know. I never read his book, and the chances are a hundred to one I never will. But I thought you might know."

"I don't. The hospital got pretty excited about the book's being published. They laid their fears on Sherwin and his possible action. But, yes, Kearnes could have tracked the whole story down. There would be ways for a clever reporter to uncover such a secret."

Mathilda pressed her napkin to her lips. Dan had been a clever reporter. Again she felt the soft, wistful grief his death had wrapped about her.

"I was trying to remember," she said, "something he told me the night he took me to dinner and told me about his book. I was upset that the little I'd told him had caused him to write the book. He was persuading me that I should not take the blame or the credit. And he said . . ." She tried hard to remember.

243

"Perhaps he was quoting from something he had read, but he said enough to convince me that night that this is the way these things happen. His book, his death, and all of it. He said that most reporters drop a pebble into a domestic pool and write about the splash. But the novelist waits, and from the vantage point of memory—I remember his saying just that!—from the vantage point of memory, he recalls the ever-widening rings of ripples that slowly subside as if nothing had disturbed the surface. He said a novelist peels away the layers of the past and finds some small thing—like Mr. Sherwin's walk on the hospital grounds, or a family dinner, or maybe just any morning's early walk—can start the whole thing, can serve as the dropped stone. Thereafter comes the implication of lives changed, misdirected, and sometimes ruined."

Brook watched her and listened. Then he stood up and held his hand out to her. "Dan did some overly deep peeling," he said gruffly.

Again, as they left the dining room and went out into the hall, they spoke to people. "Will Mrs. Bailey be going home soon?" Mathilda asked him, as if they had talked about such things all during the past hour.

"In a week. After a month or two, we'll try again. We are pretty sure the anaesthesia was her problem. Some people are more sensitive than others."

"I do hope it works out," said Mathilda. "I hope *everything* works out!" She spoke very tensely.

They had reached the elevators and were waiting. "It will," said Brook. "Everything will work. Tomorrow you and I will get our blood tests and go downtown for the

244

license. On Monday, we can get married. And that will work out, too."

"I don't see how it can," said Mathilda. "I don't see how you can go on yelling at me in o.r."

He considered this. "You're right," he agreed. "You'll have to quit your job. And I hate like hell to break in a new scrub."

Mathilda giggled. "All bets are off then?"

"No-no," said Brook, letting her precede him into the elevator. "I'm just warning you. You had better make the whole thing worthwhile."

The door closed; they were alone, and would be for twenty seconds. His strong arm drew her close, and he kissed her—hard. "Mind what I say," he said as they felt the cage slow, and he released her.

She touched his cheek with her hand. "Oh, yes, Doctor," she said happily. "Of *course,* Doctor!"